MW00577853

Praise for *All of the Belles*

"How wonderful to have Sally Carrol, Nancy, and Ailie together in this smart new collection! All three were Southern belles who understood quite well the complexities of their time and place. In these stories they will live on and on and delight a new generation of readers." — JAMES L. W. WEST III, General Editor Emeritus, Cambridge Fitzgerald Edition

"*All of the Belles* is an extraordinary gift, not only to devotees of Zelda and Scott Fitzgerald but readers, historians, and book-lovers everywhere. Dr. Kirk Curnutt's masterful introduction alone is worth the price, providing not only a refresher course in the enduring mystique of the Fitzgeralds but also a reminder of Zelda's profound influence on Scott's work. Although the stories of this collection are tender and lyrical on the surface, the underlying theme of change and loss brands them as uniquely Fitzgerald." — CASSANDRA KING, author of *Tell Me a Story: My Life with Pat Conroy*

"A revelatory read for Fitzgerald fans and Southern studies buffs alike. *All of the Belles* is beautifully drawn. In these pages, the modern belle was born. Invaluable insights into both Zelda and Scott are here represented in stories of Southern folkways and mores, encountered by both Fitzgeralds during their mythic time in Montgomery." — LEE SMITH, author of *Guests on Earth* and *Fair and Tender Ladies*

"F. Scott Fitzgerald's three stories set in the fictional Southern town of Tarleton depict the contrast between North and South (most evident in the figure of the Southern belle—the author's tribute to his wife, Zelda) and exemplify Fitzgerald's theme of love frustrated by social boundaries. Gathered together here for the first time, along with Kirk Curnutt's authoritative and graceful introduction, they evocatively show Fitzgerald's evolution from youthful romanticism in 'The Ice Palace' to disenchantment in 'The Jelly-Bean' to the mature understanding of reality in 'The Last of the Belles.'" — JACKSON R. BRYER, President of The F. Scott Fitzgerald Society

ALL OF THE BELLES

The Montgomery Stories of F. Scott Fitzgerald

F. SCOTT FITZGERALD

WITH AN INTRODUCTION BY KIRK CURNUTT

NEWSOUTH BOOKS

Montgomery

NewSouth Books
105 S. Court Street
Montgomery, AL 36104

© 2020 by NewSouth Books. Introduction © 2020 by Kirk Curnutt.
All rights reserved under International and Pan-American Copyright
Conventions. Published in the United States by NewSouth Books,
Montgomery, Alabama.
"The Last of the Belles," from *Taps at Reveille, Short Stories by F. Scott
Fitzgerald.* Copyright © 1935 by Charles Scribner's Sons. Copyright
(c) 1971 by Charles Scribner's Sons. Reprinted with the permission of
Scribner, a division of Simon & Schuster, Inc.
All rights reserved.

Library of Congress Cataloging-in-Publication Data

Names: Fitzgerald, F. Scott (Francis Scott), 1896-1940, author. |
Curnutt, Kirk, writer of introduction.
Title: All of the belles : the Montgomery stories of F. Scott Fitzgerald /
F. Scott Fitzgerald, ; introduction by Kirk Curnutt.
Other titles: Montgomery stories of F. Scott Fitzgerald | Ice palace.
Identifiers: LCCN 2019047447 | ISBN 9781588384232 (hardback)
Subjects: LCSH: Young women—Fiction. | Debutantes—Fiction. | Sex
role—Fiction. | Short stories, American. | Southern States—Social life
and customs—Fiction. | Montgomery (Ala.)—Fiction.
Classification: LCC PS3511.I9 A6 2020 | DDC 813/.52—dc23
LC record available at https://lccn.loc.gov/2019047447

Design by Randall Williams

Printed in the United States of America by Maple Press

NewSouth Books: Suzanne La Rosa, publisher; Randall Williams, editor-in-
chief; Lisa Emerson, accounting manager; Lisa Harrison, publicist; Matthew
Byrne, production manager; Beth Marino, senior publicity/marketing
manager; Kelly Snyder and Isabella Barrera, editorial and publicity assistants.

*The Black Belt, defined by its dark, rich soil, stretches across central
Alabama. It was the heart of the cotton belt. It was and is a place of
great beauty, of extreme wealth and grinding poverty, of pain and joy.
Here we take our stand, listening to the past, looking to the future.*

Contents

Introduction

"Including of course a girl . . ."

IN OCTOBER 1919, F. Scott Fitzgerald embarked on a euphoric train ride to Montgomery, Alabama. He had made what he thought was his last trip to the dusty, dowdy Southern capital five months earlier when his eighteen-year-old girlfriend, the local belle Zelda Sayre, unceremoniously refused his hand in marriage. If that mad dash had left the former Army lieutenant brokenhearted, this visit would be triumphant. In Scott's pocket was a letter from Charles Scribner's Sons accepting his debut novel *This Side of Paradise*. The firm had twice declined the book the previous fall, around the same time he and Zelda shared their first kiss as he trained for the Great War alongside thirty thousand other soldiers of the 9th Infantry Division at nearby Camp Sheridan. The rejection was a setback he'd never prepared for; from an early age his natural gift with words had assured him literary renown was written in the stars.

For Fitzgerald, becoming a famous author and winning the woman of his dreams were intertwined ambitions. He would never convince Zelda he could finance the adventurous lives they both pined for without his name in print, for writing was the only profession he was reasonably suited for. By the same token, literary success would be meaningless without her by his side. Zelda had inspired at least one sassy debutante in *Paradise,* and whole passages from her poetic letters had found their way into his prose. Editor Maxwell Perkins had no sooner sent word that Scribner's was prepared to launch his career than Fitzgerald requested they go to press as quickly as possible. "Would it be utterly impossible for you to publish the book Xmas—or say by February?" he begged. "I have so many things dependent on its success—including of course a girl. . . ."

When his train pulled into Union Station, an ornate Romanesque landmark that still sits on a scenic bluff above the Alabama River, Zelda was excited but leery. Montgomery was a provincial, cloistered city, and while she was bored with dance recitals and country-club socials, she also worried whether her audacity would stand out as boldly outside the confines of her sheltered Southern world, or whether Scott's success would make her a mere accessory to his talent. To entertain her beau—and perhaps to keep him out of sight of the local boys she dated, who taunted the invading Midwesterner as "F. *Scotch* Fitzgerald"—she squired him to one of her favorite hangouts: Oakwood Cemetery, a burial ground older than the town itself where hundreds of Civil War casualties rest.

As Fitzgerald recalled less than a year later, Zelda "told me I could never understand how she felt about the Confederate graves, and I told her that I understood so well I could put it on paper."

Returning home to St. Paul, Minnesota, with a promise that a wedding would indeed accompany his novel's publication, he dashed off a nearly ten-thousand-word short story called "The Ice Palace." Set partly in a fictional version of Montgomery called Tarleton that he relocated across the state border to Georgia (probably so he didn't offend his future wife's hometown), the tale starred a Zelda-esque heroine named Sally Carrol Happer and featured witty repartee, dreamy bursts of description, and a long, delicious French kiss rather provocatively stolen among Oakwood's "wavy valley" of Johnny Reb headstones.

The story was one of a half-dozen whimsical romances Fitzgerald cranked out in the six months between his mission to Montgomery and April 3, 1920, the day he and Zelda officially wed in the rectory of St. Patrick's Cathedral in New York City. The ceremony took place exactly one week after *This Side of Paradise* hit bookstores, less than a year since Zelda had broken off their original romance. Not only were his tales of young love adorning the pages of *The Saturday Evening Post,* the most widely read magazine of the day, but already he and Zelda were garnering mention in gossip columns and literary editorials as glamorous representatives of "the rising generation." Love and literature would never again seem so divinely fated, nor so intensely synonymous.

When Fitzgerald soon gathered the tales he wrote in this period in *Flappers and Philosophers,* his first collection of short fiction, reviewers singled out "The Ice Palace" for praise. As with its sister selections, the tale possesses a hallucinatory quality that contributes mightily to its charm. When Sally Carrol travels from Tarleton to frosty Minnesota to meet her Yankee fiancé's family, she gets lost among the translucent corridors of a towering Xanadu-like castle inspired by similar structures Fitzgerald remembered his fellow St. Paulians building out of ice blocks during the harsh winters of 1916 and 1917. To survive the tundra, the young woman calls upon her guardian spirit: a postbellum belle buried in Oakwood named Margery Lee. The scorching heat of Tarleton may slow life to a snail's pace, the story says, but at least emotions broil as humidly as the weather. The passions never go frigid as they do in the North. Sally Carrol's vision of Margery Lee, inspired by her creator's love of Romantic poetry like Samuel Taylor Coleridge's "Kubla Khan" and John Keats's "La Belle Dame Sans Merci," reminds us how essential fantasy was to F. Scott Fitzgerald's sensibility. Other stories written while he pursued Zelda take place on desert islands where flappers deliver romantic manifestos as unspoiled by actuality as the paradises around them, or among the jazz cabarets and vaudeville spectacles of New York City nightlife, where theatricality becomes a form of self-invention that electrifies life into performance art.

Yet when Fitzgerald set a second story in Tarleton a few months into his marriage, it was with a new, bittersweet sense of realism. This was the flip side of his mindset, the awareness that dreams are easily dashed, that the imagination is as fragile as it is powerful. In "The Jelly-Bean" the hero is a townie, Jim Powell, so stymied by a lack of motivation and opportunity that he is stereotyped as a "corner loafer," the type of slacker "who spends his life conjugating the verb to idle in the first person singular—I am idling, I have idled, I will idle." The only thing in Tarleton that sparks Jim's fire is Nancy Lamar, a friend of Sally Carrol's with "a mouth like a remembered kiss," who "left a trail of broken hearts from Atlanta to New Orleans." In other words, another Zelda.

Because Jim is considered a "running mate of poor whites," he is an outsider among Tarleton's popular clique, not quite up to socioeconomic snuff to imagine himself a suitable beau for Nancy. In this way, as many critics have noted, "The Jelly-Bean" reiterates the recurring plot of Fitzgerald's fiction—an impoverished young man tries to prove himself worthy of a golden girl whose affection promises entry into a world of enchantment and wealth. You may remember this as the premise of a little book called *The Great Gatsby*. As Jim strikes up an unlikely friendship with Nancy, he tries to protect her from the temptations of alcohol and gambling newly available to modern girls, as well as from cads like Ogden Merritt, a rich jerk from Savannah whose daddy's money comes from a razor-blade empire. Although "The Jelly-Bean" is a tale of unrequited love (the "unrequited" part thrown into confusion thanks to yet another deep kiss, a Fitzgerald trademark), it also dramatizes a characteristic not as widely celebrated: its author's sympathy for the plight of belles like Nancy and Sally Carrol, who want to break free from the rigid sex roles of the South but lack viable role models for carrying their revolt into adulthood. Fitzgerald always claimed his personality was more feminine than masculine. Like most sensitive men who fancy themselves poets, he idealized women, placing them on impossible pedestals, but he cheered on their rebellion while wondering aloud—sometimes paternalistically—how they would reconcile their spunk with motherhood and marriage. In "The Jelly-Bean," though, instead of Sally Carrol's Southern warmth and vivacity, the parching Fahrenheit in Tarleton represents the stagnation of small-town status quos. "All life was weather," Jim decides, "a waiting through the hot where events had no significance for the cool that was soft and caressing like a woman's hand on a tired forehead."

As Fitzgerald wrote "The Jelly-Bean" he briefly toyed with setting more stories in Tarleton. By the time he included the story in his second collection, *Tales of the Jazz Age* (1922), he decided he didn't want to be pigeonholed by a Southern setting. He continued spinning variations on his near-loss of Zelda, mixed with memories of earlier romantic humiliations he'd suffered. (While a Princeton student, he'd pursued the Lake Forest, Illinois, debutante Ginevra King. He claimed that while visiting her in 1916 he overheard a wealthy family member mutter, "Poor boys shouldn't think of marrying rich girls"—a snub that also stuck with him.) Instead of a fictional Montgomery, he might set 1922's "Winter Dreams" around Minnesota's White Bear Lake or 1924's "'The Sensible

Thing'" in southern Tennessee. Even the flashbacks in *The Great Gatsby* to the soldier/belle romance between Jay Gatsby and Daisy Fay relocate Alabama's capital to Louisville, Kentucky, home to a different military training installation that Fitzgerald passed through on his way to Camp Sheridan. Only in 1929 did he return to his wife's hometown for a final visit to Tarleton; it would prove the saddest and loveliest of the three stories.

The very title "The Last of the Belles" conveys the loss that is the DNA of Fitzgerald's most characteristic work. Years after the end of the Great War, a narrator known only as Andy recalls his attraction to yet another Zelda figure: the queen of Tarleton's aristocratic sisterhood, Ailie Calhoun. The story aches with nostalgia for the heady chaos that the influx of soldiers at Camp Sheridan brought to Montgomery as they nearly doubled its population; it also regrets the ways that chaos has become the norm in the time since Andy, like Fitzgerald, made it as far as the embarkation point to the Western Front before the Armistice denied him the opportunity to prove his mettle in combat. (A few years later Fitzgerald wrote another story with the blunt title "I Didn't Get Over.") At certain points, as when Andy refers to some Army officers as having "queer names without vowels in them," "Belles" can seem elitist and nativist in bemoaning the promotion of enlisted men from non-Anglo immigrant backgrounds into the leadership ranks. Yet overall the story sings the pervasive lament that the war brought change without delivering purpose or direction. The decade separating

"The Ice Palace" and "The Jelly-Bean" from "The Last of the Belles," of course, was the Roaring Twenties, heralded even in its own time for its frantic but stylish rudderlessness. By the time Fitzgerald wrote this final Tarleton installment, he could see the era's "ain't we got fun" ethos rapidly spiraling into neuroses and madness, its spendthrift love of leisure, fashion, and entertainment into rampant profligacy and outright fraud. The Fitzgeralds themselves were on the cusp of marital and financial ruin, gazing into the maw of alcoholism and mental illness but incapable of finding in each other either salve or security.

Like Andy, Ailie in the story's present-day scenes seems like a soldier in a revolution whose rewards have passed her by. For one thing—unlike most Montgomery women of Zelda's clique—she has never married, though rumor has her perpetually engaged to a series of ever more plebeian men, none of whom really understand her or Tarleton as Andy claims to. ("I suppose that poetry is a Northern man's dream of the South," reads the story's most famous line.) For another, she remains as intoxicatingly beautiful and effervescent as she did at eighteen, despite the "half-laughing, half-desperate banter of the newer South" she has adopted, which is designed to "leave no time for thinking—the present, the future, herself, me."

In essence, "The Last of the Belles" is Fitzgerald's admission that his generation had come of age without growing up. In the absence of a mature acceptance of the fleetingness of romance, all Andy can do is kick through the "knee-deep underbrush" where the long-gone military camp once stood, "looking for my youth in a clapboard or a strip of roofing or a rusty tomato can." One can argue that Fitzgerald was a little hard on himself and his generation. He was all of thirty-two when he wrote the story, an age when plenty of people are still uncertain about what aging and adulthood mean. Still, few writers ever appealed as eloquently to the human need to mourn the passing of time and the stages of life as Fitzgerald did. Like the best of his work, "The Last of the Belles," which he collected in his final story collection, *Taps at Reveille* (1935), rhapsodizes melancholy into cathartic uplift—exactly the consolation that artful language should give us.

Over the many decades now since F. Scott Fitzgerald has been posthumously celebrated as one of America's greatest writers, his three Tarleton tales have been reprinted in various anthologies and compilations alongside other examples of the 160-plus short stories he published throughout his twenty-year career. *All of the Belles* marks the first time the trio has been presented as a trilogy or triptych. We do so in honor of the hundredth anniversary of Scott and Zelda's marriage and to launch centennial celebrations of the first, most exuberant stage of his career. Those celebrations begin with the recent anniversary of Maxwell Perkins's September 16, 1919, letter accepting *This Side of Paradise* and will lead up to April 10, 2025, when *The Great Gatsby* turns one hundred.

All of the Belles also insists that the Tarleton stories are best appreciated as a complete artistic statement, a fitting tribute to Zelda's hometown. Montgomery is a city notoriously scarred by paradoxes and contradictions reflective of larger wounds America has yet to heal. Most obviously, the state capitol where Jefferson Davis declared the South's secession from the Union stares down upon the Dexter Avenue King Memorial Baptist Church where Martin Luther King Jr. and other members of the Montgomery Bus Boycott began the long fight to dismantle segregation.

The Fitzgeralds are part of this history, even if in romanticizing the South they were silently indifferent to the horrors of slavery and lynching, never condemning the racism of the Ku Klux Klan or of the white power structure with the moral fervor William Faulkner did when he transformed Oxford, Mississippi, into Yoknapatawpha County. (Zelda's father, Anthony Dickinson Sayre, a state legislator and Supreme Court of Alabama justice, played an influential role in shaping the 1901 constitution, which explicitly disenfranchised African Americans in Alabama.) The real-life sites these stories allude to sat on the same downtown blocks where battle lines over Civil War and civil rights were drawn a century apart. Most of Scott and Zelda's haunts were razed long ago, a perfect metaphor for how their love story sometimes ends up erased by the more epochal events the city grapples with in its ongoing struggle to make peace with its dual identity. The country club where they met—a central setting in "The Jelly-Bean"—is now home to a Sonic Drive-In. Nothing remains of Camp Sheridan but a couple of cannons and a marker. The "strangely shabby and stuffy" Jefferson Hotel where Andy stays when he visits Tarleton, officially the Jefferson *Davis* Hotel, has long been converted into a Social Security home for the elderly and disabled. Oakwood Cemetery remains virtually unchanged for lovers who want to reenact Sally Carrol's kiss there, and the house at 919 Felder Avenue where the couple briefly lived in 1931–1932 has survived for more than thirty years as home to the Scott and Zelda Fitzgerald Museum, recently expanding into an Airbnb where fans can rest as if sleeping off a Jazz Age bender. For the most part, though, tracing Scott and Zelda's footsteps in Montgomery requires knowing these three tales of restless belles. Without them, like Andy, we're left kicking the underbrush, looking for remnants.

Recently one startling juxtaposition has dramatized more powerfully than ever before the value of reading these stories as part of the larger, bloodier history that Montgomery, the South, and America in general have borne. In April 2018 the Equal Justice Initiative, a high-profile social justice and legal reform non-profit led by attorney Bryan Stevenson, opened the National Memorial for Peace and Justice on six acres of abandoned land slightly west of downtown. Dedicated to victims of racial terrorism from slavery through Jim Crow into our own era of police shootings and judicial bias, the memorial comprises eight hundred hanging steel columns, each engraved with the names of black men and women lynched in a particular American county. To stroll the descending walkway that gradually raises the columns above one's head is a wrenching ritual of both humility and complicity. It bows us to the overwhelming truth, still so often brushed under the rug or outright denied, of how many lives were lost to the

violence of white supremacy. The brilliant design also leaves
the viewer in the uncomfortable position of gazing up at the
victims, many of them simply recorded as "Unknown," just as
many of the gawkers who attended lynchings gazed up at the
"strange fruit hanging from the poplar trees." Greeting visitors
as they emerge from the grisly roll call is a quote from Toni
Morrison that reads in part: "And O my people, out yonder,
hear me, they do not love your neck unnoosed and straight.
So love your neck; put a hand on it, grace it, stroke it and hold
it up. And all your inside parts that they'd just as soon slop
for hogs, you got to love them." The source is unidentified,
but a literature teacher will recognize it immediately. It's a
passage from *Beloved*, one of the few literary masterpieces
that, by virtue of its uncompromising insistence on the right
to memorialize atrocities against African Americans, can
make a serious claim to being a *Greater* American Novel
than *The Great Gatsby*.

But for Fitzgerald fans the truly unnerving moment
comes strolling along the memorial's south side, where one
encounters a street named Pleasant Avenue, which should
ring a bell. It was here, a few houses down, that Zelda grew
up at number six. Photographs galore capture her sweeping
its steps, posing in her mother's rose garden in a ballet costume before a ball, sitting with Scott in the back yard. The
images correspond to the description of the sunlight-dappled
house in "The Ice Palace" where Sally Carrol Happer pouts in
languor, and of the "four white pillars of the Calhoun house"
that "faced the street, and behind them the verandah . . . dark

as a cave with hanging, weaving, climbing vines" where Andy watches fellow camp officers compete to court Ailie in "The Last of the Belles."

Unfortunately, nothing remains of the Fitzgeralds at 6 Pleasant Avenue. The lot has sat empty since the mid-1970s, when the house was condemned and torn down after years of abandonment. There isn't even a marker to note the literary significance of the location. Nobody has ever bothered to put one up because visitors rarely turn down the weed-choked, impoverished cul-de-sac, not even a fraction of the four hundred thousand tourists the lynching memorial drew to Montgomery in its first year alone.

Not surprisingly, there is nothing of Scott and Zelda inside the memorial either, which is appropriate. A literary historian can track down the column for the Lafayette County in Mississippi where Faulkner lived most of his life and read the name of Nelse Patton, whose 1908 lynching inspired the gruesome execution of Joe Christmas in *Light in August* (1932), or that of Elwood Higginbotham, whose 1935 death at the hands of an Oxford mob led to *Intruder in the Dust* (1948). Yet the Tarleton stories take place in a sanitized, privileged Montgomery where there is no whisper of Miles (or Relius) Phifer and Robert Crosky, two black veterans of the Great War hunted down in the woods outside the city on phony charges of assaulting white women, or of John Temple, shot dead in a hospital ward after killing a white policeman in a scuffle. All three were murdered on September 29–30, 1919, as Scott planned the trip that would inspire "The Ice Palace." Their deaths were part of a nationwide wave of white-supremacist violence known as Red Summer, which Fitzgerald never wrote about.

The only thing connecting the lynching memorial to Pleasant Avenue is an intervening strip of east-west asphalt called Mildred Street. Although the road isn't abnormally wide, stand on either side and the gulf between these two places only fifty yards apart seems insurmountable. There just feels like no honest way to bridge the gap between unimaginable black suffering and delicate white poignancy, between historical crime and literary beauty, between Toni Morrison and F. Scott Fitzgerald. Yet as Fitzgerald himself once wrote, "The test of a first-rate intelligence is the ability to hold two opposed ideas in mind at the same time and still retain the ability to function." Too often we want to reconcile incongruous chapters of history, forcing the pieces to fit to convince ourselves we can solve the puzzle and make it whole. Contrast can be as illuminating as unity, though. It reminds us that the friction generated along the border between two incompatible things prevents us from oversimplifying the stories we tell. And if the story of Zelda's hometown deserves anything, it's not to have its contradictions artificially resolved.

All of the Belles gathers three stories of the South then that don't mention the things the South is most famous for. Fitzgerald's Tarleton tales are about entitled young women bucking against convention and discovering that new freedoms perhaps aren't so freeing. Until some ambitious creative writer produces an epic tale that somehow synthesizes the black and white history of central Alabama, the trio will stand as the best, most polished fiction about Montgomery, a city that few creative writers have ever had the courage to take on precisely because its history is so momentous. Because the stories are key to appreciating how thoroughly Zelda fascinated her husband, giving his imagination focus and shape, they demonstrate that Fitzgerald understood the South by understanding her. Toward the end of his life, he remembered the desperation he felt trying to prove his art was the ticket to their shared yearning for extraordinary lives: "I was in love with a whirlwind and I must spin a net big enough to catch it out of my head," he wrote, "a head full of trickling nickels and sliding dimes, the incessant music box of the poor."

Reading "The Ice Palace," "The Jelly-Bean," and "The Last of Belles" in sequence shows he didn't have to cast that net wide to spin it rich.

— KIRK CURNUTT

Kirk Curnutt is executive director of the F. Scott Fitzgerald Society and serves as managing editor of The F. Scott Fitzgerald Review. *He is professor and chair of English at Troy University.*

All of the Belles

The Ice Palace

The Saturday Evening Post, 22 May 1920

THE SUNLIGHT dripped over the house like golden paint over an art jar, and the freckling shadows here and there only intensified the rigor of the bath of light. The Butterworth and Larkin houses flanking were intrenched behind great stodgy trees; only the Happer house took the full sun and all day long faced the dusty road-street with a tolerant kindly patience. This was the city of Tarleton in southernmost Georgia—September afternoon.

Up in her bedroom window Sally Carrol Happer rested her nineteen-year-old chin on a fifty-two-year-old sill and watched Clark Darrow's ancient Ford turn the corner. The car was hot—being partly metallic it retained all the heat it absorbed or evolved—and Clark Darrow sitting bolt upright at the wheel wore a pained, strained expression as though he considered himself a spare part and rather likely to break. He laboriously crossed two dust ruts, the wheels squeaking indignantly at the encounter, and then with a terrifying expression he gave the steering-gear a final wrench and deposited self and car approximately in front of the Happer steps. There was a plaintive heaving sound, a death-rattle, followed by a short silence; and then the air was rent by a startling whistle.

Sally Carrol gazed down sleepily. She started to yawn, but finding this quite impossible unless she raised her chin from the window-sill, changed her mind and continued silently to regard the car, whose owner sat brilliantly if perfunctorily at attention as he waited for an answer to his signal. After a moment the whistle once more split the dusty air.

"Good mawnin'."

With difficulty Clark twisted his tall body round and bent a distorted glance on the window.

"'Tain't mawnin', Sally Carrol."

"Isn't it, sure enough?"

"What you doin'?"

"Eatin' 'n apple."

"Come on go swimmin'—want to?"

"Reckon so."

"How 'bout hurryin' up?"

"Sure enough."

Sally Carrol sighed voluminously and raised herself with profound inertia from the floor, where she had been occupied in alternately destroying parts of a green apple and painting paper dolls for her younger sister. She approached a mirror, regarded her expression with a pleased and pleasant languor, dabbed two spots of rouge on her lips and a grain of powder on her nose and covered her bobbed corn-colored hair with a rose-littered sunbonnet. Then she kicked over the painting water, said, "Oh, damn!"—but let it lie—and left the room.

"How you, Clark?" she inquired a minute later as she slipped nimbly over the side of the car.

"Mighty fine, Sally Carrol."

"Where we go swimmin'?"

"Out to Walley's Pool. Told Marylyn we'd call by an' get her an' Joe Ewing."

Clark was dark and lean and when on foot was rather inclined to stoop. His eyes were ominous and his expression somewhat petulant except when startlingly illuminated by one of his frequent smiles. Clark had "a income"—just enough to keep himself in ease and his car in gasoline—and he had spent the two years since he graduated from Georgia Tech in dozing round the lazy streets of his home town, discussing how he could best invest his capital for an immediate fortune.

Hanging round he found not at all difficult; a crowd of little girls had grown up beautifully, the amazing Sally Carrol foremost among them; and they enjoyed being swum with and danced with and made love to in the flower-filled summery evenings—and they all liked Clark immensely. When feminine company palled there were half a dozen other youths who were always just about to do something, and meanwhile were quite willing to join him in a few holes of golf, or a game of billiards, or the consumption of a quart of "hard yella licker." Every once in awhile one of these contemporaries made a farewell round of calls before going up to New York or Philadelphia or Pittsburgh to go into business, but mostly they just stayed round in this languid paradise of dreamy skies and firefly evenings and noisy niggery street fairs—and especially of gracious soft-voiced girls, who were brought up on memories instead of money.

The Ford having been excited into a sort of restless resentful life Clark and Sally Carrol rolled and rattled down Valley Avenue into Jefferson Street, where the dust road became a pavement; along opiate Millicent Place, where there were half a dozen prosperous substantial mansions; and on into the downtown section. Driving was perilous here, for it was shopping time; the population idled casually across the streets and a drove of low-moaning oxen were being urged along in front of a placid street-car; even the shops seemed only yawning their doors and blinking their windows in the sunshine before retiring into a state of utter and finite coma.

"Sally Carrol," said Clark suddenly, "it a fact that you're engaged?"

She looked at him quickly.

"Where'd you hear that?"

"Sure enough, you engaged?"

"'At's a nice question!"

"Girl told me you were engaged to a Yankee you met up in Asheville last summer."

Sally Carrol sighed.

"Never saw such an old town for rumors."

"Don't marry a Yankee, Sally Carrol. We need you round here."

Sally Carrol was silent a moment.

"Clark," she demanded suddenly, "who on earth shall I marry?"

"I offer my services."

"Honey, you couldn't support a wife," she answered cheerfully. "Anyway, I know you too well to fall in love with you."

"'At doesn't mean you ought to marry a Yankee," he persisted.

"S'pose I love him?"

He shook his head.

"You couldn't. He'd be a lot different from us, every way." He broke off as he halted the car in front of a rambling, dilapidated house. Marylyn Wade and Joe Ewing appeared in the doorway.

"'Lo, Sally Carrol."

"Hi!"

"How you-all?"

"Sally Carrol," demanded Marylyn as they started off again, "you engaged?"

"Lawdy, where'd all this start? Can't I look at a man 'thout everybody in town engagin' me to him?"

Clark stared straight in front of him at a bolt on the clattering windshield.

"Sally Carrol," he said with a curious intensity, "don't you like us?"

"What?"

"Us down here?"

"Why, Clark, you know I do. I adore all you boys."

"Then why you gettin' engaged to a Yankee?"

"Clark, I don't know. I'm not sure what I'll do, but—well, I want to go places and see people. I want my mind to grow.

I want to live where things happen on a big scale."

"What you mean?"

"Oh, Clark, I love you, and I love Joe here, and Ben Arrot, and you-all, but you'll—you'll——"

"We'll all be failures?"

"Yes. I don't mean only money failures, but just sort of—of ineffectual and sad, and—oh, how can I tell you?"

"You mean because we stay here in Tarleton?"

"Yes, Clark; and because you like it and never want to change things or think or go ahead."

He nodded and she reached over and pressed his hand.

"Clark," she said softly, "I wouldn't change you for the world. You're sweet the way you are. The things that'll make you fail I'll love always—the living in the past, the lazy days and nights you have, and all your carelessness and generosity."

"But you're goin' away?"

"Yes—because I couldn't ever marry you. You've a place in my heart no one else ever could have, but tied down here I'd get restless. I'd feel I was—wastin' myself. There's two sides to me, you see. There's the sleepy old side you love; an' there's a sort of energy—the feelin' that makes me do wild things. That's the part of me that may be useful somewhere, that'll last when I'm not beautiful anymore."

She broke off with characteristic suddenness and sighed, "Oh, sweet cooky!" as her mood changed.

Half-closing her eyes and tipping back her head till it rested on the seat-back she let the savory breeze fan her eyes and ripple the fluffy curls of her bobbed hair. They were in the country now, hurrying between tangled growths of bright-green coppice and grass and tall trees that sent sprays of foliage to hang a cool welcome over the road. Here and there they passed a battered negro cabin, its oldest white-haired inhabitant smoking a corncob pipe beside the door and half a dozen scantily clothed pickaninnies parading tattered dolls on the wild-grown grass in front. Farther out were lazy cotton fields, where even the workers seemed intangible shadows lent by the sun to the earth not for toil but to while away some age-old tradition in the golden September fields. And round the drowsy picturesqueness, over the trees and shacks and muddy rivers, flowed the heat, never hostile, only comforting like a great warm nourishing bosom for the infant earth.

"Sally Carrol, we're here!"

"Poor chile's soun' asleep."

"Honey, you dead at last outa sheer laziness?"

"Water, Sally Carrol! Cool water waitin' for you!"

Her eyes opened sleepily.

"Hi!" she murmured, smiling.

II

In November Harry Bellamy, tall, broad, and brisk, came down from his Northern city to spend four days. His intention was to settle a matter that had been hanging fire since he and Sally Carrol had met in Asheville, North Carolina, in midsummer. The settlement took only a quiet afternoon and an evening in front of a glowing open fire, for Harry Bellamy had everything she wanted; and, besides,

9

ALL OF THE BELLES

she loved him—loved him with that side of her she kept especially for loving. Sally Carrol had several rather clearly defined sides.

On his last afternoon they walked, and she found their steps tending half-unconsciously toward one of her favorite haunts, the cemetery. When it came in sight, gray-white and golden-green under the cheerful late sun, she paused irresolute by the iron gate.

"Are you mournful by nature, Harry?" she asked with a faint smile.

"Mournful? Not I."

"Then let's go in here. It depresses some folks, but I like it."

They passed through the gateway and followed a path that led through a wavy valley of graves—dusty-gray and moldy for the fifties; quaintly carved with flowers and jars for the seventies; ornate and hideous for the nineties, with fat marble cherubs lying in sodden sleep on stone pillows, and great impossible growths of nameless granite flowers. Occasionally they saw a kneeling figure with tributary flowers, but over most of the graves lay silence and withered leaves with only the fragrance that their own shadowy memories could waken in living minds.

They reached the top of a hill where they were fronted by a tall, round headstone, freckled with dark spots of damp and half grown over with vines.

"Margery Lee," she read; "1844–1873. Wasn't she nice? She died when she was twenty-nine. Dear Margery Lee," she added softly. "Can't you see her, Harry?"

"Yes, Sally Carrol."

He felt a little hand insert itself into his.

"She was dark, I think; and she always wore her hair with a ribbon in it, and gorgeous hoop-skirts of alice blue and old rose."

"Yes."

"Oh, she was sweet, Harry! And she was the sort of girl born to stand on a wide pillared porch and welcome folks in. I think perhaps a lot of men went away to war meanin' to come back to her; but maybe none of 'em ever did."

He stooped down close to the stone, hunting for any record of marriage.

"There's nothing here to show."

"Of course not. How could there be anything there better than just 'Margery Lee,' and that eloquent date?"

She drew close to him and an unexpected lump came into his throat as her yellow hair brushed his cheek.

"You see how she was, don't you, Harry?"

"I see," he agreed gently. "I see through your precious eyes. You're beautiful now, so I know she must have been."

Silent and close they stood, and he could feel her shoulders trembling a little. An ambling breeze swept up the hill and stirred the brim of her floppidy hat.

"Let's go down there!"

She was pointing to a flat stretch on the other side of the hill where along the green turf were a thousand grayish-white crosses stretching in endless ordered rows like the stacked arms of a battalion.

"Those are the Confederate dead," said Sally Carrol simply.

They walked along and read the inscriptions, always only a name and a date, sometimes quite indecipherable.

"The last row is the saddest—see, 'way over there. Every cross has just a date on it and the word 'Unknown.'"

She looked at him and her eyes brimmed with tears.

"I can't tell you how real it is to me, darling—if you don't know."

"How you feel about it is beautiful to me."

"No, no, it's not me, it's them—that old time that I've tried to have live in me. These were just men, unimportant evidently or they wouldn't have been 'unknown'; but they died for the most beautiful thing in the world—the dead South. You see," she continued, her voice still husky, her eyes glistening with tears, "people have these dreams they fasten onto things, and I've always grown up with that dream. It was so easy because it was all dead and there weren't any disillusions comin' to me. I've tried in a way to live up to those past standards of noblesse oblige—there's just the last remnants of it, you know, like the roses of an old garden dying all round us—streaks of strange courtliness and chivalry in some of these boys an' stories I used to hear from a Confederate soldier who lived next door, and a few old darkies. Oh, Harry, there was something, there was something! I couldn't ever make you understand, but it was there."

"I understand," he assured her again quietly.

Sally Carrol smiled and dried her eyes on the tip of a handkerchief protruding from his breast pocket.

"You don't feel depressed, do you, lover? Even when I cry I'm happy here, and I get a sort of strength from it."

Hand in hand they turned and walked slowly away. Finding soft grass she drew him down to a seat beside her with their backs against the remnants of a low broken wall.

"Wish those three old women would clear out," he complained. "I want to kiss you, Sally Carrol."

"Me, too."

They waited impatiently for the three bent figures to move off, and then she kissed him until the sky seemed to fade out and all her smiles and tears to vanish in an ecstasy of eternal seconds.

Afterward they walked slowly back together, while on the corners twilight played at somnolent black-and-white checkers with the end of day.

"You'll be up about mid-January," he said, "and you've got to stay a month at least. It'll be slick. There's a winter carnival on, and if you've never really seen snow it'll be like fairyland to you. There'll be skating and skiing and tobogganing and sleigh-riding and all sorts of torchlight parades on snowshoes. They haven't had one for years, so they're going to make it a knock-out."

"Will I be cold, Harry?" she asked suddenly.

"You certainly won't. You may freeze your nose, but you won't be shivery cold. It's hard and dry, you know."

"I guess I'm a summer child. I don't like any cold I've ever seen."

She broke off and they were both silent for a minute.

"Sally Carrol," he said very slowly, "what do you say to—March?"

"I say I love you."

"March?"

"March, Harry."

III

All night in the Pullman it was very cold. She rang for the porter to ask for another blanket, and when he couldn't give her one she tried vainly, by squeezing down into the bottom of her berth and doubling back the bedclothes, to snatch a few hours' sleep. She wanted to look her best in the morning.

She rose at six and sliding uncomfortably into her clothes stumbled up to the diner for a cup of coffee. The snow had filtered into the vestibules and covered the floor with a slippery coating. It was intriguing, this cold, it crept in everywhere. Her breath was quite visible and she blew into the air with a naïve enjoyment. Seated in the diner she stared out the window at white hills and valleys and scattered pines whose every branch was a green platter for a cold feast of snow. Sometimes a solitary farmhouse would fly by, ugly and bleak and lone on the white waste; and with each one she had an instant of chill compassion for the souls shut in there waiting for spring.

As she left the diner and swayed back into the Pullman she experienced a surging rush of energy and wondered if she was feeling the bracing air of which Harry had spoken. This was the North, the North—her land now!

"Then blow, ye winds, heigho!

A-roving I will go,"

she chanted exultantly to herself.

"What's 'at?" inquired the porter politely.

"I said: 'Brush me off.'"

The long wires of the telegraph poles doubled; two tracks ran up beside the train—three—four; came a succession of white-roofed houses, a glimpse of a trolley car with frosted windows, streets—more streets—the city.

She stood for a dazed moment in the frosty station before she saw three fur-bundled figures descending upon her.

"There she is!"

"Oh, Sally Carrol!"

Sally Carrol dropped her bag.

"Hi!"

A faintly familiar icy-cold face kissed her, and then she was in a group of faces all apparently emitting great clouds of heavy smoke; she was shaking hands. There were Gordon, a short, eager man of thirty who looked like an amateur knocked-about model for Harry, and his wife, Myra, a listless lady with flaxen hair under a fur automobile cap. Almost immediately Sally Carrol thought of her as vaguely Scandinavian. A cheerful chauffeur adopted her bag, and amid ricochets of half-phrases, exclamations, and perfunctory listless "my dears" from Myra, they swept each other from the station.

Then they were in a sedan bound through a crooked succession of snowy streets where dozens of little boys were hitching sleds behind grocery wagons and automobiles.

"Oh," cried Sally Carrol, "I want to do that! Can we, Harry?"

"That's for kids. But we might——"

"It looks like such a circus!" she said regretfully.

Home was a rambling frame house set on a white lap of snow, and there she met a big, gray-haired man of whom she approved, and a lady who was like an egg and who kissed her—these were Harry's parents. There was a breathless indescribable hour crammed full of half-sentences, hot water, bacon and eggs and confusion; and after that she was alone with Harry in the library, asking him if she dared smoke.

It was a large room with a Madonna over the fireplace and rows upon rows of books in covers of light gold and dark gold and shiny red. All the chairs had little lace squares where one's head should rest, the couch was just comfortable, the books looked as if they had been read—some—and Sally Carrol had an instantaneous vision of the battered old library at home with her father's huge medical books and the oil paintings of her three great-uncles and the old couch that had been mended up for forty-five years and was still luxurious to dream in. This room struck her as being neither attractive nor particularly otherwise. It was simply a room with a lot of fairly expensive things in it that all looked about fifteen years old.

"What do you think of it up here?" demanded Harry eagerly. "Does it surprise you? Is it what you expected, I mean?"

"You are, Harry," she said quietly, and reached out her arms to him.

But after a brief kiss he seemed anxious to extort enthusiasm from her.

"The town, I mean. Do you like it? Can you feel the pep in the air?"

"Oh, Harry," she laughed, "you'll have to give me time. You can't just fling questions at me."

She puffed at her cigarette with a sigh of contentment.

"One thing I want to ask you," he began rather apologetically; "you Southerners put quite an emphasis on family and all that—not that it isn't quite all right, but you'll find it a little different here. I mean—you'll notice a lot of things that'll seem to you sort of vulgar display at first, Sally Carrol; but just remember that this is a three-generation town. Everybody has a father and about half of us have grandfathers. Back of that we don't go."

"Of course," she murmured.

"Our grandfathers, you see, founded the place, and a lot of them had to take some pretty queer jobs while they were doing the founding. For instance, there's one woman who at present is about the social model for the town; well, her father was the first public ash man—things like that."

"Why," said Sally Carrol, puzzled, "did you s'pose I was goin' to make remarks about people?"

"Not at all," interrupted Harry; "and I'm not apologizing for anyone either. It's just that—well, a Southern girl came up here last summer and said some unfortunate things, and—oh, I just thought I'd tell you."

Sally Carrol felt suddenly indignant—as though she had

been unjustly spanked—but Harry evidently considered the subject closed, for he went on with a great surge of enthusiasm.

"It's carnival time, you know. First in ten years. And there's an ice palace they're building now that's the first they've had since eighty-five. Built out of blocks of the clearest ice they could find—on a tremendous scale."

She rose and walking to the window pushed aside the heavy Turkish portières and looked out.

"Oh!" she cried suddenly. "There's two little boys makin' a snowman! Harry, do you reckon I can go out an' help 'em?"

"You dream! Come here and kiss me."

She left the window rather reluctantly.

"I don't guess this is a very kissable climate, is it? I mean, it makes you so you don't want to sit round, doesn't it?"

"We're not going to. I've got a vacation for the first week you're here, and there's a dinner-dance tonight."

"Oh, Harry," she confessed, subsiding in a heap, half in his lap, half in the pillows, "I sure do feel confused. I haven't got an idea whether I'll like it or not, an' I don't know what people expect or anythin'. You'll have to tell me, honey."

"I'll tell you," he said softly, "if you'll just tell me you're glad to be here."

"Glad—just awful glad!" she whispered, insinuating herself into his arms in her own peculiar way. "Where you are is home for me, Harry."

And as she said this she had the feeling for almost the first time in her life that she was acting a part.

That night, amid the gleaming candles of a dinner party

where the men seemed to do most of the talking while the girls sat in a haughty and expensive aloofness, even Harry's presence on her left failed to make her feel at home.

"They're a good-looking crowd, don't you think?" he demanded. "Just look round. There's Spud Hubbard, tackle at Princeton last year, and Junie Morton—he and the red-haired fellow next to him were both Yale hockey captains; Junie was in my class. Why, the best athletes in the world come from these states round here. This is a man's country, I tell you. Look at John J. Fishburn!"

"Who's he?" asked Sally Carrol innocently.

"Don't you know?"

"I've heard the name."

"Greatest wheat man in the Northwest, and one of the greatest financiers in the country."

She turned suddenly to a voice on her right.

"I guess they forgot to introduce us. My name's Roger Patton."

"My name is Sally Carrol Happer," she said graciously.

"Yes, I know. Harry told me you were coming."

"You a relative?"

"No, I'm a professor."

"Oh," she laughed.

"At the university. You're from the South, aren't you?"

"Yes; Tarleton, Georgia."

She liked him immediately—a reddish-brown mustache under watery blue eyes that had something in them that these other eyes lacked, some quality of appreciation. They exchanged stray sentences through dinner and she made up her mind to see him again.

After coffee she was introduced to numerous good-looking young men who danced with conscious precision and seemed to take it for granted that she wanted to talk about nothing except Harry.

"Heavens," she thought, "they talk as if my being engaged made me older than they are—as if I'd tell their mothers on them!"

In the South an engaged girl, even a young married woman, expected the same amount of half-affectionate badinage and flattery that would be accorded a debutante, but here all that seemed banned. One young man, after getting well started on the subject of Sally Carrol's eyes and how they had allured him ever since she entered the room, went into a violent confusion when he found she was visiting the Bellamys—was Harry's fiancée. He seemed to feel as though he had made some risqué and inexcusable blunder, became immediately formal, and left her at the first opportunity.

She was rather glad when Roger Patton cut in on her and suggested that they sit out a while.

"Well," he inquired, blinking cheerily, "how's Carmen from the South?"

"Mighty fine. How's—how's Dangerous Dan McGrew? Sorry, but he's the only Northerner I know much about."

He seemed to enjoy that.

"Of course," he confessed, "as a professor of literature I'm not supposed to have read Dangerous Dan McGrew."

"Are you a native?"

"No, I'm a Philadelphian. Imported from Harvard to teach French. But I've been here ten years."

"Nine years, three hundred an' sixty-four days longer than me."

"Like it here?"

"Uh-huh. Sure do!"

"Really?"

"Well, why not? Don't I look as if I were havin' a good time?"

"I saw you look out the window a minute ago—and shiver."

"Just my imagination," laughed Sally Carrol. "I'm used to havin' everythin' quiet outside, an' sometimes I look out an' see a flurry of snow, an' it's just as if somethin' dead was movin'."

He nodded appreciatively.

"Ever been North before?"

"Spent two Julys in Asheville, North Carolina."

"Nice-looking crowd, aren't they?" suggested Patton, indicating the swirling floor.

Sally Carrol started. This had been Harry's remark.

"Sure are! They're—canine."

"What?"

She flushed.

"I'm sorry; that sounded worse than I meant it. You see I always think of people as feline or canine, irrespective of sex."

"Which are you?"

"I'm feline. So are you. So are most Southern men an' most of these girls here."

"What's Harry?"

"Harry's canine distinctly. All the men I've met tonight seem to be canine."

"What does 'canine' imply? A certain conscious masculinity as opposed to subtlety?"

"Reckon so. I never analyzed it—only I just look at people an' say 'canine' or 'feline' right off. It's right absurd, I guess."

"Not at all. I'm interested. I used to have a theory about these people. I think they're freezing up."

"What?"

"I think they're growing like Swedes—Ibsenesque, you know. Very gradually getting gloomy and melancholy. It's these long winters. Ever read any Ibsen?"

She shook her head.

"Well, you find in his characters a certain brooding rigidity. They're righteous, narrow, and cheerless, without infinite possibilities for great sorrow or joy."

"Without smiles or tears?"

"Exactly. That's my theory. You see there are thousands of Swedes up here. They come, I imagine, because the climate is very much like their own, and there's been a gradual mingling. There're probably not half a dozen here tonight, but—we've had four Swedish governors. Am I boring you?"

"I'm mighty interested."

"Your future sister-in-law is half Swedish. Personally I like her, but my theory is that Swedes react rather badly on us as a whole. Scandinavians, you know, have the largest suicide rate in the world."

"Why do you live here if it's so depressing?"

"Oh, it doesn't get me. I'm pretty well cloistered, and I suppose books mean more than people to me anyway."

"But writers all speak about the South being tragic. You know—Spanish señoritas, black hair and daggers an' haunting music."

He shook his head.

"No, the Northern races are the tragic races—they don't indulge in the cheering luxury of tears."

Sally Carrol thought of her graveyard. She supposed that that was vaguely what she had meant when she said it didn't depress her.

"The Italians are about the gayest people in the world—but it's a dull subject," he broke off. "Anyway, I want to tell you you're marrying a pretty fine man."

Sally Carrol was moved by an impulse of confidence.

"I know. I'm the sort of person who wants to be taken care of after a certain point, and I feel sure I will be."

"Shall we dance? You know," he continued as they rose, "it's encouraging to find a girl who knows what she's marrying for. Nine-tenths of them think of it as a sort of walking into a moving-picture sunset."

She laughed, and liked him immensely.

Two hours later on the way home she nestled near Harry in the back seat.

"Oh, Harry," she whispered, "it's so co-old!"

"But it's warm in here, darling girl."

"But outside it's cold; and oh, that howling wind!"

She buried her face deep in his fur coat and trembled

involuntarily as his cold lips kissed the tip of her ear.

IV

The first week of her visit passed in a whirl. She had her promised toboggan ride at the back of an automobile through a chill January twilight. Swathed in furs she put in a morning tobogganing on the country-club hill; even tried skiing, to sail through the air for a glorious moment and then land in a tangled laughing bundle on a soft snowdrift. She liked all the winter sports, except an afternoon spent snow-shoeing over a glaring plain under pale yellow sunshine, but she soon realized that these things were for children—that she was being humored and that the enjoyment round her was only a reflection of her own.

At first the Bellamy family puzzled her. The men were reliable and she liked them; to Mr. Bellamy especially, with his iron-gray hair and energetic dignity, she took an immediate fancy, once she found that he was born in Kentucky; this made of him a link between the old life and the new. But toward the women she felt a definite hostility. Myra, her future sister-in-law, seemed the essence of spiritless conventionality. Her conversation was so utterly devoid of personality that Sally Carrol, who came from a country where a certain amount of charm and assurance could be taken for granted in the women, was inclined to despise her.

"If those women aren't beautiful," she thought, "they're nothing. They just fade out when you look at them. They're glorified domestics. Men are the center of every mixed group."

Lastly there was Mrs. Bellamy, whom Sally Carrol detested. The first day's impression of an egg had been confirmed—an egg with a cracked, veiny voice and such an ungracious dumpiness of carriage that Sally Carrol felt that if she once fell she would surely scramble. In addition, Mrs. Bellamy seemed to typify the town in being innately hostile to strangers. She called Sally Carrol "Sally," and could not be persuaded that the double name was anything more than a tedious ridiculous nickname. To Sally Carrol this shortening of her name was like presenting her to the public half-clothed. She loved "Sally Carrol"; she loathed "Sally." She knew also that Harry's mother disapproved of her bobbed hair; and she had never dared smoke downstairs after that first day when Mrs. Bellamy had come into the library sniffing violently.

Of all the men she met she preferred Roger Patton, who was a frequent visitor at the house. He never again alluded to the Ibsenesque tendency of the populace, but when he came in one day and found her curled upon the sofa bent over "Peer Gynt" he laughed and told her to forget what he'd said—that it was all rot.

And then one afternoon in her second week she and Harry hovered on the edge of a dangerously steep quarrel. She considered that he precipitated it entirely, though the Serbia in the case was an unknown man who had not had his trousers pressed.

They had been walking homeward between mounds of high-piled snow and under a sun which Sally Carrol scarcely recognized. They passed a little girl done up in gray wool until she resembled a small Teddy bear, and Sally Carrol could not resist a gasp of maternal appreciation.

"Look! Harry!"

"What?"

"That little girl—did you see her face?"

"Yes, why?"

"It was red as a little strawberry. Oh, she was cute!"

"Why, your own face is almost as red as that already! Everybody's healthy here. We're out in the cold as soon as we're old enough to walk. Wonderful climate!"

She looked at him and had to agree. He was mighty healthy-looking; so was his brother. And she had noticed the new red in her own cheeks that very morning.

Suddenly their glances were caught and held and they stared for a moment at the street corner ahead of them. A man was standing there, his knees bent, his eyes gazing upward with a tense expression as though he were about to make a leap toward the chilly sky. And then they both exploded into a shout of laughter, for coming closer they discovered it had been a ludicrous momentary illusion produced by the extreme bagginess of the man's trousers.

"Reckon that's one on us," she laughed.

"He must be a Southerner, judging by those trousers," suggested Harry mischievously.

"Why, Harry!"

Her surprised look must have irritated him.

"Those damn Southerners!"

Sally Carrol's eyes flashed.

"Don't call 'em that!"

"I'm sorry, dear," said Harry, malignantly apologetic, "but you know what I think of them. They're sort of—sort of degenerates—not at all like the old Southerners. They've lived so long down there with all the colored people that they've gotten lazy and shiftless."

"Hush your mouth, Harry!" she cried angrily. "They're not! They may be lazy—anybody would be in that climate—but they're my best friends, an' I don't want to hear 'em criticized in any such sweepin' way. Some of 'em are the finest men in the world."

"Oh, I know. They're all right when they come North to college, but of all the hangdog, ill-dressed, slovenly lot I ever saw, a bunch of small-town Southerners are the worst!"

Sally Carrol was clinching her gloved hands and biting her lip furiously.

"Why," continued Harry, "there was one in my class at New Haven and we all thought that at last we'd found the true type of Southern aristocrat, but it turned out that he wasn't an aristocrat at all—just the son of a Northern carpetbagger who owned about all the cotton round Mobile."

"A Southerner wouldn't talk the way you're talking now," she said evenly.

"They haven't the energy!"

"Or the somethin' else."

"I'm sorry, Sally Carrol, but I've heard you say yourself that you'd never marry——"

"That's quite different. I told you I wouldn't want to tie

my life to any of the boys that are round Tarleton now, but I never made any sweepin' generalities."

They walked along in silence.

"I probably spread it on a bit thick, Sally Carrol. I'm sorry."

She nodded but made no answer. Five minutes later as they stood in the hallway she suddenly threw her arms round him.

"Oh, Harry," she cried, her eyes brimming with tears, "let's get married next week. I'm afraid of having fusses like that. I'm afraid, Harry. It wouldn't be that way if we were married."

But Harry, being in the wrong, was still irritated.

"That'd be idiotic. We decided on March."

The tears in Sally Carrol's eyes faded; her expression hardened slightly.

"Very well—I suppose I shouldn't have said that."

Harry melted.

"Dear little nut!" he cried. "Come and kiss me and let's forget."

That very night at the end of a vaudeville performance the orchestra played "Dixie" and Sally Carrol felt something stronger and more enduring than her tears and smiles of the day brim up inside her. She leaned forward gripping the arms of her chair until her face grew crimson.

"Sort of get you, dear?" whispered Harry.

But she did not hear him. To the spirited throb of the violins and the inspiring beat of the kettledrums her own old ghosts were marching by and on into the darkness, and as fifes whistled and sighed in the low encore they seemed so nearly out of sight that she could have waved good-bye.

"Away, Away,
　Away down South in Dixie!
Away, away,
　Away down South in Dixie!"

V

It was a particularly cold night. A sudden thaw had nearly cleared the streets the day before, but now they were traversed again with a powdery wraith of loose snow that traveled in wavy lines before the feet of the wind and filled the lower air with a fine-particled mist. There was no sky—only a dark, ominous tent that draped in the tops of the streets and was in reality a vast approaching army of snowflakes—while over it all, chilling away the comfort from the brown-and-green glow of lighted windows and muffling the steady trot of the horse pulling their sleigh, interminably washed the north wind. It was a dismal town after all, she thought—dismal.

Sometimes at night it had seemed to her as though no one lived here—they had all gone long ago—leaving lighted houses to be covered in time by tombing heaps of sleet. Oh, if there should be snow on her grave! To be beneath great piles of it all winter long, where even her headstone would be a light shadow against light shadows. Her grave—a grave that should be flower-strewn and washed with sun and rain.

She thought again of those isolated country houses that her train had passed, and of the life there the long winter through—the ceaseless glare through the windows, the crust forming on the soft drifts of snow, finally the slow, cheerless melting and the harsh spring of which Roger Patton had told her. Her spring—to lose it forever—with its lilacs and the lazy sweetness it stirred in her heart. She was laying away that spring—afterward she would lay away that sweetness.

With a gradual insistence the storm broke. Sally Carrol felt a film of flakes melt quickly on her eyelashes and Harry reached over a furry arm and drew down her complicated flannel cap. Then the small flakes came in skirmish line and the horse bent his neck patiently as a transparency of white appeared momentarily on his coat.

"Oh, he's cold, Harry," she said quickly.

"Who? The horse? Oh, no, he isn't. He likes it!"

After another ten minutes they turned a corner and came in sight of their destination. On a tall hill outlined in vivid glaring green against the wintry sky stood the ice palace. It was three stories in the air, with battlements and embrasures and narrow icicled windows, and the innumerable electric lights inside made a gorgeous transparency of the great central hall. Sally Carrol clutched Harry's hand under the fur robe.

"It's beautiful!" he cried excitedly. "My golly, it's beautiful, isn't it! They haven't had one here since eighty-five!"

Somehow the notion of there not having been one since eighty-five oppressed her. Ice was a ghost, and this mansion of it was surely peopled by those shades of the eighties, with pale faces and blurred snow-filled hair.

"Come on, dear," said Harry.

She followed him out of the sleigh and waited while he hitched the horse. A party of four—Gordon, Myra, Roger

Patton, and another girl—drew up beside them with a mighty jingle of bells. There was quite a crowd already, bundled in fur or sheepskin, shouting and calling to each other as they moved through the snow, which was now so thick that people could scarcely be distinguished a few yards away.

"It's a hundred and seventy feet tall," Harry was saying to a muffled figure beside him as they trudged toward the entrance; "covers six thousand square yards."

She caught snatches of conversation: "One main hall"— "walls twenty to forty inches thick"—"and the ice cave has almost a mile of—"—"this Canuck who built it——"

They found their way inside, and dazed by the magic of the great crystal walls Sally Carrol found herself repeating over and over two lines from "Kubla Khan":

> "It was a miracle of rare device,
> A sunny pleasure-dome with caves of ice!"

In the great glittering cavern with the dark shut out she took a seat on a wooden bench, and the evening's oppression lifted. Harry was right—it was beautiful; and her gaze traveled the smooth surface of the walls, the blocks for which had been selected for their purity and clearness to obtain this opalescent, translucent effect.

"Look! Here we go—oh, boy!" cried Harry.

A band in a far corner struck up "Hail, Hail, the Gang's All Here!" which echoed over to them in wild muddled acoustics, and then the lights suddenly went out; silence seemed to flow down the icy sides and sweep over them. Sally Carrol could still see her white breath in the darkness, and a dim row of pale faces over on the other side.

The music eased to a sighing complaint, and from outside drifted in the full-throated resonant chant of the marching clubs. It grew louder like some pæan of a viking tribe traversing an ancient wild; it swelled—they were coming nearer; then a row of torches appeared, and another and another, and keeping time with their moccasined feet a long column of gray-mackinawed figures swept in, snow-shoes slung at their shoulders, torches soaring and flickering as their voices rose along the great walls.

The gray column ended and another followed, the light streaming luridly this time over red toboggan caps and flaming crimson mackinaws, and as they entered they took up the refrain; then came a long platoon of blue and white, of green, of white, of brown and yellow.

"Those white ones are the Wacouta Club," whispered Harry eagerly. "Those are the men you've met round at dances."

The volume of the voices grew; the great cavern was a phantasmagoria of torches waving in great banks of fire, of colors and the rhythm of soft-leather steps. The leading column turned and halted, platoon deployed in front of platoon until the whole procession made a solid flag of flame, and then from thousands of voices burst a mighty shout that filled the air like a crash of thunder and sent the torches wavering. It was magnificent, it was tremendous! To Sally Carrol it was the North offering sacrifice on some mighty altar to the gray pagan God of Snow. As the shout died the band struck up again and there came more singing, and then long reverberating cheers by each club. She sat very quiet listening while the staccato cries rent the stillness; and then she started, for there was a volley of explosion, and great clouds of smoke went up here and there through the cavern—the flash-light photographers at work—and the council was over. With the band at their head the clubs formed in column once more, took up their chant, and began to march out.

"Come on!" shouted Harry. "We want to see the labyrinths down-stairs before they turn the lights off!"

They all rose and started toward the chute—Harry and Sally Carrol in the lead, her little mitten buried in his big fur gauntlet. At the bottom of the chute was a long empty room of ice with the ceiling so low that they had to stoop—and their hands were parted. Before she realized what he intended Harry had darted down one of the half-dozen glittering passages that opened into the room and was only a vague receding blot against the green shimmer.

"Harry!" she called.

"Come on!" he cried back.

She looked round the empty chamber; the rest of the party had evidently decided to go home, were already outside somewhere in the blundering snow. She hesitated and then darted in after Harry.

"Harry!" she shouted.

She had reached a turning point thirty feet down; she

heard a faint muffled answer far to the left, and with a touch of panic fled toward it. She passed another turning, two more yawning alleys.

"Harry!"

No answer. She started to run straight forward, and then turned like lightning and sped back the way she had come, enveloped in a sudden icy terror.

She reached a turn—was it here?—took the left and came to what should have been the outlet into the long, low room, but it was only another glittering passage with darkness at the end. She called again, but the walls gave back a flat, lifeless echo with no reverberations. Retracing her steps she turned another corner, this time following a wide passage. It was like the green lane between the parted waters of the Red Sea, like a damp vault connecting empty tombs.

She slipped a little now as she walked, for ice had formed on the bottom of her overshoes; she had to run her gloves along the half-slippery, half-sticky walls to keep her balance.

"Harry!"

Still no answer. The sound she made bounced mockingly down to the end of the passage.

Then on an instant the lights went out and she was in complete darkness. She gave a small frightened cry and sank down into a cold little heap on the ice. She felt her left knee do something as she fell, but she scarcely noticed it as some deep terror far greater than any fear of being lost settled upon her. She was alone with this presence that came out of the North, the dreary loneliness that rose from ice-bound whalers in the Arctic seas, from smokeless trackless wastes where were strewn the whitened bones of adventure. It was an icy breath of death; it was rolling down low across the land to clutch at her.

With a furious despairing energy she rose again and started blindly down the darkness. She must get out. She might be lost in here for days, freeze to death and lie embedded in the ice like corpses she had read of, kept perfectly preserved until the melting of a glacier. Harry probably thought she had left with the others—he had gone by now; no one would know until late next day. She reached pitifully for the wall. Forty inches thick, they had said—forty inches thick!

"Oh!"

On both sides of her along the walls she felt things creeping, damp souls that haunted this palace, this town, this North.

"Oh, send somebody—send somebody!" she cried aloud.

Clark Darrow—he would understand; or Joe Ewing; she couldn't be left here to wander forever—to be frozen, heart, body, and soul. This her—this Sally Carrol! Why, she was a happy thing. She was a happy little girl. She liked warmth and summer and Dixie. These things were foreign—foreign.

"You're not crying," something said aloud. "You'll never cry any more. Your tears would just freeze; all tears freeze up here!"

She sprawled full length on the ice.

"Oh, God!" she faltered.

A long single file of minutes went by, and with a great weariness she felt her eyes closing. Then someone seemed to sit down near her and take her face in warm, soft hands. She looked up gratefully.

"Why, it's Margery Lee," she crooned softly to herself. "I knew you'd come." It really was Margery Lee, and she was just as Sally Carrol had known she would be, with a young white brow and wide welcoming eyes and a hoop-skirt of some soft material that was quite comforting to rest on.

"Margery Lee."

It was getting darker now and darker—all those tomb-stones ought to be repainted, sure enough, only that would spoil 'em, of course. Still, you ought to be able to see 'em.

Then after a succession of moments that went fast and then slow, but seemed to be ultimately resolving themselves into a multitude of blurred rays converging toward a pale yellow sun, she heard a great cracking noise break her new-found stillness.

It was the sun, it was a light; a torch, and a torch beyond that, and another one, and voices; a face took flesh below the torch, heavy arms raised her, and she felt something on her cheek—it felt wet. Someone had seized her and was rubbing her face with snow. How ridiculous—with snow!

"Sally Carrol! Sally Carrol!"

It was Dangerous Dan McGrew; and two other faces she didn't know.

"Child, child! We've been looking for you two hours! Harry's half-crazy!"

Things came rushing back into place—the singing, the torches, the great shout of the marching clubs. She squirmed in Patton's arms and gave a long low cry.

"Oh, I want to get out of here! I'm going back home. Take me home"—her voice rose to a scream that sent a chill to Harry's heart as he came racing down the next passage—"tomorrow!" she cried with delirious, unrestrained passion—"Tomorrow! Tomorrow! Tomorrow!"

VI

The wealth of golden sunlight poured a quite enervating yet oddly comforting heat over the house where day-long it faced the dusty stretch of road. Two birds were making a great to-do in a cool spot found among the branches of a tree next door, and down the street a colored woman was announcing herself melodiously as a purveyor of strawberries. It was April afternoon.

Sally Carrol Happer, resting her chin on her arm and her arm on an old window seat, gazed sleepily down over the spangled dust whence the heat waves were rising for the first time this spring. She was watching a very ancient Ford turn a perilous corner and rattle and groan to a jolting stop at the end of the walk. She made no sound, and in a minute a strident familiar whistle rent the air. Sally Carrol smiled and blinked.

"Good mawnin'."

A head appeared tortuously from under the car top below.

"'Tain't mawnin', Sally Carrol."

"Sure enough!" she said in affected surprise. "I guess maybe not."

"What you doin'?"

"Eatin' green peach. 'Spect to die any minute."

Clark twisted himself a last impossible notch to get a view of her face.

"Water's warm as a kettla steam, Sally Carrol. Wanta go swimmin'?"

"Hate to move," sighed Sally Carrol lazily, "but I reckon so."

The Jelly-Bean

The Metropolitan, October 1920

JIM POWELL was a Jelly-bean. Much as I desire to make him an appealing character, I feel that it would be unscrupulous to deceive you on that point. He was a bred-in-the-bone, dyed-in-the-wool, ninety-nine three-quarters per cent Jelly-bean and he grew lazily all during Jelly-bean season, which is every season, down in the land of the Jelly-beans well below the Mason-Dixon line.

Now if you call a Memphis man a Jelly-bean he will quite possibly pull a long sinewy rope from his hip pocket and hang you to a convenient telegraph pole. If you call a New Orleans man a Jelly-bean he will probably grin and ask you who is taking your girl to the Mardi Gras ball. The particular Jelly-bean patch which produced the protagonist of this history lies somewhere between the two—a little city of forty thousand that has dozed sleepily for forty thousand years in southern Georgia, occasionally stirring in its slumbers and muttering something about a war that took place sometime, somewhere, and that everyone else has forgotten long ago.

Jim was a Jelly-bean. I write that again because it has

such a pleasant sound—rather like the beginning of a fairy story—as if Jim were nice. It somehow gives me a picture of him with a round, appetizing face and all sorts of leaves and vegetables growing out of his cap. But Jim was long and thin and bent at the waist from stooping over pool-tables, and he was what might have been known in the indiscriminating North as a corner loafer. "Jelly-bean" is the name throughout the undissolved Confederacy for one who spends his life conjugating the verb to idle in the first person singular—I am idling, I have idled, I will idle.

Jim was born in a white house on a green corner. It had four weather-beaten pillars in front and a great amount of lattice-work in the rear that made a cheerful criss-cross background for a flowery sun-drenched lawn. Originally the dwellers in the white house had owned the ground next door and next door to that and next door to that, but this had been so long ago that even Jim's father scarcely remembered it. He had, in fact, thought it a matter of so little moment that when he was dying from a pistol wound got in a brawl he neglected even to tell little Jim, who was five years old and miserably frightened. The white house became a boarding house run by a tight-lipped lady from Macon, whom Jim called Aunt Mamie and detested with all his soul.

He became fifteen, went to high school, wore his hair in black snarls, and was afraid of girls. He hated his home where four women and one old man prolonged an interminable chatter from summer to summer about what lots the Powell place had originally included and what sort of flowers would be out next. Sometimes the parents of little girls in town, remembering Jim's mother and fancying a resemblance in the dark eyes and hair, invited him to parties, but parties made him shy and he much preferred sitting on a disconnected axle in Tilly's garage, rolling the bones or exploring his mouth endlessly with a long straw. For pocket money, he picked up odd jobs, and it was due to this that he stopped going to parties. At his third party little Marjorie Haight had whispered indiscreetly and within hearing distance that he was a boy who brought the groceries sometimes. So instead of the two-step and polka, Jim had learned to throw any number he desired on the dice and had listened to spicy tales of all the shootings that had occurred in the surrounding country during the past fifty years.

He became eighteen. The war broke out and he enlisted as a gob and polished brass in the Charleston Navy Yard for a year. Then, by way of variety, he went north and polished brass in the Brooklyn Navy Yard for a year.

When the war was over he came home. He was twenty-one, his trousers were too short and too tight. His buttoned shoes were long and narrow. His tie was an alarming conspiracy of purple and pink marvelously scrolled, and over it were two blue eyes faded like a piece of very good old cloth long exposed to the sun.

In the twilight of one April evening when a soft gray had drifted down along the cotton fields and over the sultry town, he was a vague figure leaning against a board fence, whistling and gazing at the moon's rim above the lights of Jackson

Street. His mind was working persistently on a problem that had held his attention for an hour. The Jelly-bean had been invited to a party.

Back in the days when all the boys had detested all the girls, Clark Darrow and Jim had sat side by side in school. But, while Jim's social aspirations had died in the oily air of the garage, Clark had alternately fallen in and out of love, gone to college, taken to drink, given it up, and, in short, become one of the best beaux of the town. Nevertheless Clark and Jim had retained a friendship that, though casual, was perfectly definite. That afternoon Clark's ancient Ford had slowed up beside Jim, who was on the sidewalk and, out of a clear sky, Clark had invited him to a party at the country club. The impulse that made him do this was no stranger than the impulse which made Jim accept. The latter was probably an unconscious ennui, a half-frightened sense of adventure. And now Jim was soberly thinking it over.

He began to sing, drumming his long foot idly on a stone block in the sidewalk till it wobbled up and down in time to the low throaty tune:

> "One mile from Home in Jelly-bean town,
> Lives Jeanne, the Jelly-bean Queen.
> She loves her dice and treats 'em nice;
> No dice would treat her mean."

He broke off and agitated the sidewalk to a bumpy gallop. "Daggone!" he muttered, half-aloud.

They would all be there—the old crowd, the crowd to which, by right of the white house, sold long since, and the portrait of the officer in gray over the mantel, Jim should have belonged. But that crowd had grown up together into a tight little set as gradually as the girls' dresses had lengthened inch by inch, as definitely as the boys' trousers had dropped suddenly to their ankles. And to that society of first names and dead puppy-loves Jim was an outsider—a running mate of poor whites. Most of the men knew him, condescendingly; he tipped his hat to three or four girls. That was all.

When the dusk had thickened into a blue setting for the moon, he walked through the hot, pleasantly pungent town to Jackson Street. The stores were closing and the last shoppers were drifting homeward, as if borne on the dreamy revolution of a slow merry-go-round. A street-fair farther down made a brilliant alley of varicolored booths and contributed a blend of music to the night—an oriental dance on a calliope, a melancholy bugle in front of a freak show, a cheerful rendition of "Back Home in Tennessee" on a hand-organ.

The Jelly-bean stopped in a store and bought a collar. Then he sauntered along toward Soda Sam's, where he found the usual three or four cars of a summer evening parked in front and the little darkies running back and forth with sundaes and lemonades.

"Hello, Jim."

It was a voice at his elbow—Joe Ewing sitting in an automobile with Marylyn Wade. Nancy Lamar and a strange man were in the back seat.

The Jelly-bean tipped his hat quickly.

"Hi, Ben—" then, after an almost imperceptible pause—"How y' all?"

Passing, he ambled on toward the garage where he had a room upstairs. His "How y'all" had been said to Nancy Lamar, to whom he had not spoken in fifteen years.

Nancy had a mouth like a remembered kiss and shadowy eyes and blue-black hair inherited from her mother who had been born in Budapest. Jim passed her often in the street, walking small-boy fashion with her hands in her pockets and he knew that with her inseparable Sally Carrol Happer she had left a trail of broken hearts from Atlanta to New Orleans.

For a few fleeting moments Jim wished he could dance. Then he laughed and as he reached his door began to sing softly to himself:

> "Her Jelly-Roll can twist your soul,
> Her eyes are big and brown,
> She's the Queen of the Queens of the Jelly-beans—
> My Jeanne of Jelly-bean Town."

II

At nine-thirty Jim and Clark met in front of Soda Sam's and started for the country club in Clark's Ford.

"Jim," asked Clark casually, as they rattled through the jasmine-scented night, "how do you keep alive?"

The Jelly-bean paused, considered.

"Well," he said finally, "I got a room over Tilly's garage. I help him some with the cars in the afternoon an' he gives it to me free. Sometimes I drive one of his taxis and pick up a little thataway. I get fed up doin' that regular though."

"That all?"

"Well, when there's a lot of work I help him by the day—Saturdays usually—and then there's one main source of revenue I don't generally mention. Maybe you don't recollect I'm about the champion crap-shooter of this town. They make me shoot from a cup now because once I get the feel of a pair of dice they just roll for me."

Clark grinned appreciatively.

"I never could learn to set 'em so's they'd do what I wanted. Wish you'd shoot with Nancy Lamar some day and take all her money away from her. She will roll 'em with the boys and she loses more than her daddy can afford to give her. I happen to know she sold a good ring last month to pay a debt."

The Jelly-bean was noncommittal.

"The white house on Elm Street still belong to you?"

Jim shook his head.

"Sold. Got a pretty good price, seein' it wasn't in a good part of town no more. Lawyer told me to put it into Liberty bonds. But Aunt Mamie got so she didn't have no sense, so it takes all the interest to keep her up at Great Farms Sanitarium."

"Hm."

"I got an old uncle upstate an' I reckin I kin go up there if ever I get sure enough pore. Nice farm, but not enough niggers around to work it. He's asked me to come up and help him, but I don't guess I'd take much to it. Too doggone lonesome——" He broke off suddenly. "Clark, I want to tell you I'm much obliged to you for askin' me out but I'd be a lot happier if you'd just stop the car right here an' let me walk back into town."

"Shucks!" Clark grunted. "Do you good to step out. You don't have to dance—just get out there on the floor and shake."

"Hold on," exclaimed Jim uneasily. "Don't you go leadin' me up to any girls and leavin' me there so I'll have to dance with 'em."

Clark laughed.

"'Cause," continued Jim desperately, "without you swear you won't do that I'm agoin' to get out right here an' my good legs goin' carry me back to Jackson Street."

They agreed after some argument that Jim, unmolested by females, was to view the spectacle from a secluded settee in the corner where Clark would join him whenever he wasn't dancing.

So ten o'clock found the Jelly-bean with his legs crossed and his arms conservatively folded, trying to look casually at home and politely uninterested in the dancers. At heart he was torn between overwhelming self-consciousness and an intense curiosity as to all that went on around him. He saw the girls emerge one by one from the dressing room, stretching and pluming themselves like bright birds, smiling over their powdered shoulders at the chaperones, casting a quick glance around to take in the room and, simultaneously, the room's reaction to their entrance—and then, again like birds, alighting and nestling in the sober arms of their waiting escorts. Sally Carrol Happer, blonde and lazy-eyed, appeared clad in her favorite pink and blinking like an awakened rose. Marjorie Haight, Marylyn Wade, Harriet Cary, all the girls he had seen loitering down Jackson Street by noon, now, curled and brilliantined and delicately tinted for the overhead lights, were miraculously strange Dresden figures of pink and blue and red and gold, fresh from the shop and not yet fully dried.

He had been there half an hour, totally uncheered by Clark's jovial visits which were each one accompanied by a "Hello, old boy, how you making out?" and a slap at his knee. A dozen males had spoken to him or stopped for a moment beside him, but he knew that they were each one surprised at finding him there and fancied that one or two were even slightly resentful. But at half past ten his embarrassment suddenly left him and a pull of breathless interest took him completely out of himself—Nancy Lamar had come out of the dressing room.

She was dressed in yellow organdie, a costume of a hundred cool corners, with three tiers of ruffles and a big bow in back until she shed black and yellow around her in a sort of phosphorescent luster. The Jelly-bean's eyes opened wide and a lump arose in his throat. For a minute she stood beside the door until her partner hurried up. Jim recognized him as the stranger who had been with her in Joe Ewing's car that afternoon. He saw her set her arms akimbo and say something in a low voice, and laugh. The man laughed too and Jim experienced the quick pang of a weird new kind of pain. Some ray had passed between the pair, a shaft of beauty from that sun that had warmed him a moment since. The Jelly-bean felt suddenly like a weed in a shadow.

A minute later Clark approached him, bright-eyed and glowing.

"Hi, old man," he cried with some lack of originality. "How you making out?"

Jim replied that he was making out as well as could be expected.

"You come along with me," commanded Clark. "I've got something that'll put an edge on the evening."

Jim followed him awkwardly across the floor and up the stairs to the locker room where Clark produced a flask of nameless yellow liquid.

"Good old corn."

Ginger ale arrived on a tray. Such potent nectar as "good old corn" needed some disguise beyond seltzer.

"Say, boy," exclaimed Clark breathlessly, "doesn't Nancy Lamar look beautiful?"

Jim nodded.

"Mighty beautiful," he agreed.

"She's all dolled up to a fare-you-well tonight," continued Clark. "Notice that fellow she's with?"

"Big fella? White pants?"

"Yeah. Well, that's Ogden Merritt from Savannah. Old man Merritt makes the Merritt safety razors. This fella's crazy about her. Been chasing after her all year.

"She's a wild baby," continued Clark, "but I like her. So does everybody. But she sure does do crazy stunts. She usually gets out alive but she's got scars all over her reputation from one thing or another she's done."

"That so?" Jim passed over his glass. "That's good corn."

"Not so bad. Oh, she's a wild one. Shoots craps, say boy! And she do like her highballs. Promised I'd give her one later on."

"She in love with this—Merritt?"

"Damned if I know. Seems like all the best girls around here marry fellas and go off somewhere."

He poured himself one more drink and carefully corked the bottle.

"Listen, Jim, I got to go dance and I'd be much obliged if you just stick this corn right on your hip as long as you're not dancing. If a man notices I've had a drink he'll come up and ask me and before I know it it's all gone and somebody else is having my good time."

So Nancy Lamar was going to marry. This toast of a town was to become the private property of an individual in white trousers—and all because white trousers' father had made a better razor than his neighbor. As they descended the stairs Jim found the idea inexplicably depressing. For the first time in his life he felt a vague and romantic yearning. A picture of her began to form in his imagination—Nancy walking boylike and debonnaire along the street, taking an orange as tithe from a worshipful fruit-dealer, charging a dope on a mythical account at Soda Sam's, assembling a convoy of beaux and then driving off in triumphal state for an afternoon of splashing and singing.

The Jelly-bean walked out on the porch to a deserted corner, dark between the moon on the lawn and the single lighted door of the ballroom. There he found a chair and, lighting a cigarette, drifted into the thoughtless reverie that was his usual mood. Yet now it was a reverie made sensuous by the night and by the hot smell of damp powder-puffs, tucked in the fronts of low dresses and distilling a thousand rich scents to float out through the open door. The music itself, blurred by a loud trombone, became hot and shadowy, a languorous overtone to the scraping of many shoes and slippers.

Suddenly the square of yellow light that fell through the door was obscured by a dark figure. A girl had come out of the dressing room and was standing on the porch not more than ten feet away. Jim heard a low-breathed "doggone" and then she turned and saw him. It was Nancy Lamar.

Jim rose to his feet.

"Howdy?"

"Hello—" she paused, hesitated, and then approached. "Oh, it's—Jim Powell."

He bowed slightly, tried to think of a casual remark.

"Do you suppose," she began quickly, "I mean—do you know anything about gum?"

"What?"

"I've got gum on my shoe. Some utter ass left his or her gum on the floor and of course I stepped in it."

Jim blushed, inappropriately.

"Do you know how to get it off?" she demanded petulantly. "I've tried a knife. I've tried every damn thing in the dressing room. I've tried soap and water—and even perfume and I've ruined my powder-puff trying to make it stick to that."

Jim considered the question in some agitation.

"Why—I think maybe gasoline——"

The words had scarcely left his lips when she grasped his hand and pulled him at a run off the low veranda, over a flower bed and at a gallop toward a group of cars parked in the moonlight by the first hole of the golf course.

"Turn on the gasoline," she commanded breathlessly.

"What?"

"For the gum of course. I've got to get it off. I can't dance with gum on."

Obediently Jim turned to the cars and began inspecting them with a view to obtaining the desired solvent. Had she demanded a cylinder he would have done his best to wrench one out.

"Here," he said after a moment's search. "Here's one that's easy. Got a handkerchief?"

"It's upstairs wet. I used it for the soap and water."

Jim laboriously explored his pockets.

"Don't believe I got one either."

"Doggone it! Well, we can turn it on and let it run on the ground."

He turned the spout; a dripping began.

"More!"

He turned it on fuller. The dripping became a flow and formed an oily pool that glistened brightly, reflecting a dozen tremulous moons on its quivering bosom.

"Ah," she sighed contentedly, "let it all out. The only thing to do is to wade in it."

In desperation he turned on the tap full and the pool suddenly widened sending tiny rivers and trickles in all directions.

"That's fine. That's something like."

Raising her skirts she stepped gracefully in.

"I know this'll take it off," she murmured.

Jim smiled.

"There's lots more cars."

She stepped daintily out of the gasoline and began scraping her slippers, side and bottom, on the running-board of the automobile. The Jelly-bean contained himself no longer. He bent double with explosive laughter and after a second she joined in.

"You're here with Clark Darrow, aren't you?" she asked as they walked back toward the veranda.

"Yes."

"You know where he is now?"

"Out dancin', I reckin."

"The deuce. He promised me a highball."

"Well," said Jim, "I guess that'll be all right. I got his bottle right here in my pocket."

She smiled at him radiantly.

"I guess maybe you'll need ginger ale though," he added.

"Not me. Just the bottle."

"Sure enough?"

She laughed scornfully.

"Try me. I can drink anything any man can. Let's sit down."

She perched herself on the side of a table and he dropped into one of the wicker chairs beside her. Taking out the cork she held the flask to her lips and took a long drink. He watched her fascinated.

"Like it?"

She shook her head breathlessly.

"No, but I like the way it makes me feel. I think most people are that way."

Jim agreed.

"My daddy liked it too well. It got him."

"American men," said Nancy gravely, "don't know how to drink."

"What?" Jim was startled.

"In fact," she went on carelessly, "they don't know how to do anything very well. The one thing I regret in my life is that I wasn't born in England."

"In England?"

"Yes. It's the one regret of my life that I wasn't."

"Do you like it over there?"

"Yes. Immensely. I've never been there in person, but I've met a lot of Englishmen who were over here in the army, Oxford and Cambridge men—you know, that's like Sewanee and University of Georgia are here—and of course I've read a lot of English novels."

Jim was interested, amazed.

"D' you ever hear of Lady Diana Manners?" she asked earnestly.

No, Jim had not.

"Well, she's what I'd like to be. Dark, you know, like me, and wild as sin. She's the girl who rode her horse up the steps of some cathedral or church or something and all the novelists made their heroines do it afterwards."

Jim nodded politely. He was out of his depths.

"Pass the bottle," suggested Nancy. "I'm going to take another little one. A little drink wouldn't hurt a baby.

"You see," she continued, again breathless after a draught. "People over there have style. Nobody has style here. I mean the boys here aren't really worth dressing up for or doing sensational things for. Don't you know?"

"I suppose so—I mean I suppose not," murmured Jim.

"And I'd like to do 'em an' all. I'm really the only girl in town that has style."

She stretched out her arms and yawned pleasantly.

"Pretty evening."

"Sure is," agreed Jim.

"Like to have boat," she suggested dreamily. "Like to sail out on a silver lake, say the Thames, for instance. Have champagne and caviare sandwiches along. Have about eight people. And one of the men would jump overboard to amuse the party and get drowned like a man did with Lady Diana Manners once."

"Did he do it to please her?"

"Didn't mean drown himself to please her. He just meant

to jump overboard and make everybody laugh."

"I reckin they just died laughin' when he drowned."

"Oh, I suppose they laughed a little," she admitted. "I imagine she did, anyway. She's pretty hard, I guess—like I am."

"You hard?"

"Like nails." She yawned again and added, "Give me a little more from that bottle."

Jim hesitated but she held out her hand defiantly.

"Don't treat me like a girl," she warned him. "I'm not like any girl *you* ever saw." She considered. "Still, perhaps you're right. You got—you got old head on young shoulders."

She jumped to her feet and moved toward the door. The Jelly-bean rose also.

"Good-bye," she said politely, "good-bye. Thanks, Jelly-bean."

Then she stepped inside and left him wide-eyed upon the porch.

III

At twelve o'clock a procession of cloaks issued single file from the women's dressing room and, each one pairing with a coated beau like dancers meeting in a cotillion figure, drifted through the door with sleepy happy laughter—through the door into the dark where autos backed and snorted and parties called to one another and gathered around the water-cooler.

Jim, sitting in his corner, rose to look for Clark. They had met at eleven; then Clark had gone in to dance. So, seeking him, Jim wandered into the soft-drink stand that had once been a bar. The room was deserted except for a sleepy negro dozing behind the counter and two boys lazily fingering a pair of dice at one of the tables. Jim was about to leave when he saw Clark coming in. At the same moment Clark looked up.

"Hi, Jim!" he commanded. "C'mon over and help us with this bottle. I guess there's not much left, but there's one all round."

Nancy, the man from Savannah, Marylyn Wade, and Joe Ewing were lolling and laughing in the doorway. Nancy caught Jim's eye and winked at him humorously.

They drifted over to a table and arranging themselves around it waited for the waiter to bring ginger ale. Jim, faintly ill at ease, turned his eyes on Nancy, who had drifted into a nickel crap game with the two boys at the next table.

"Bring them over here," suggested Clark.

Joe looked around.

"We don't want to draw a crowd. It's against club rules."

"Nobody's around," insisted Clark, "except Mr. Taylor. He's walking up and down like a wild man trying to find out who let all the gasoline out of his car."

There was a general laugh.

"I bet a million Nancy got something on her shoe again. You can't park when she's around."

"O Nancy, Mr. Taylor's looking for you!"

Nancy's cheeks were glowing with excitement over the game. "I haven't seen his silly little flivver in two weeks."

Jim felt a sudden silence. He turned and saw an individual of uncertain age standing in the doorway.

Clark's voice punctuated the embarrassment.

"Won't you join us, Mr. Taylor?"

"Thanks."

Mr. Taylor spread his unwelcome presence over a chair. "Have to, I guess. I'm waiting till they dig me up some gasoline. Somebody got funny with my car."

His eyes narrowed and he looked quickly from one to the other. Jim wondered what he had heard from the doorway—tried to remember what had been said.

"I'm right tonight," Nancy sang out, "and my four bits is in the ring."

"Faded!" snapped Taylor suddenly.

"Why, Mr. Taylor, I didn't know you shot craps!" Nancy was overjoyed to find that he had seated himself and instantly covered her bet. They had openly disliked each other since the night she had definitely discouraged a series of rather pointed advances.

"All right, babies, do it for your mamma. Just one little seven." Nancy was *cooing* to the dice. She rattled them with a brave underhand flourish, and rolled them out on the table.

"Ah-h! I suspected it. And now again with the dollar up."

Five passes to her credit found Taylor a bad loser. She was making it personal, and after each success Jim watched triumph flutter across her face. She was doubling with each throw—such luck could scarcely last.

"Better go easy," he cautioned her timidly.

"Ah, but watch this one," she whispered. It was eight on the dice and she called her number.

"Little Ada, this time we're going south."

Ada from Decatur rolled over the table. Nancy was flushed and half-hysterical, but her luck was holding. She drove the pot up and up, refusing to drag. Taylor was drumming with his fingers on the table, but he was in to stay.

Then Nancy tried for a ten and lost the dice. Taylor seized them avidly. He shot in silence, and in the hush of excitement the clatter of one pass after another on the table was the only sound.

Now Nancy had the dice again, but her luck had broken. An hour passed. Back and forth it went. Taylor had been at it again—and again and again. They were even at last—Nancy lost her ultimate five dollars.

"Will you take my check," she said quickly, "for fifty, and we'll shoot it all?" Her voice was a little unsteady and her hand shook as she reached to the money.

Clark exchanged an uncertain but alarmed glance with Joe Ewing. Taylor shot again. He had Nancy's check.

"How 'bout another?" she said wildly. "Jes' any bank'll do—money everywhere as a matter of fact."

Jim understood—the "good old corn" he had given her— the "good old corn" she had taken since. He wished he dared interfere—a girl of that age and position would hardly have two bank accounts. When the clock struck two he contained himself no longer.

"May I—can't you let me roll 'em for you?" he suggested, his low, lazy voice a little strained.

Suddenly sleepy and listless, Nancy flung the dice down before him.

"All right—old boy! As Lady Diana Manners says, 'Shoot 'em, Jelly-bean'—My luck's gone."

"Mr. Taylor," said Jim, carelessly, "we'll shoot for one of those there checks against the cash."

Half an hour later Nancy swayed forward and clapped him on the back.

"Stole my luck, you did." She was nodding her head sagely.

Jim swept up the last check and putting it with the others tore them into confetti and scattered them on the floor. Someone started singing, and Nancy kicking her chair backward rose to her feet.

"Ladies and gentlemen," she announced. "Ladies—that's you Marylyn. I want to tell the world that Mr. Jim Powell, who is a well-known Jelly-bean of this city, is an exception to a great rule—'lucky in dice—unlucky in love.' He's lucky in dice, and as matter fact I—I *love* him. Ladies and gentlemen, Nancy Lamar, famous dark-haired beauty often featured in the *Herald* as one th' most popular members of younger set as other girls are often featured in this particular case. Wish to announce—wish to announce, anyway, Gentlemen——" She tipped suddenly. Clark caught her and restored her balance.

"My error," she laughed, "she stoops to—stoops to—anyways——We'll drink to Jelly-bean . . . Mr. Jim Powell, King of the Jelly-beans."

And a few minutes later as Jim waited hat in hand for Clark in the darkness of that same corner of the porch where she had come searching for gasoline, she appeared suddenly beside him.

"Jelly-bean," she said, "are you here, Jelly-bean? I think—" and her slight unsteadiness seemed part of an enchanted dream—"I think you deserve one of my sweetest kisses for that, Jelly-bean."

For an instant her arms were around his neck—her lips were pressed to his.

"I'm a wild part of the world, Jelly-bean, but you did me a good turn."

Then she was gone, down the porch, over the cricket-loud lawn. Jim saw Merritt come out the front door and say something to her angrily—saw her laugh and, turning away, walk with averted eyes to his car. Marylyn and Joe followed, singing a drowsy song about a Jazz baby.

Clark came out and joined Jim on the steps. "All pretty lit, I guess," he yawned. "Merritt's in a mean mood. He's certainly off Nancy."

Over east along the golf course a faint rug of gray spread itself across the feet of the night. The party in the car began to chant a chorus as the engine warmed up.

"Good-night everybody," called Clark.

"Good-night, Clark."

"Good-night."

There was a pause, and then a soft, happy voice added,

"Good-night, Jelly-bean."

The car drove off to a burst of singing. A rooster on a farm across the way took up a solitary mournful crow and behind them a last negro waiter turned out the porch light. Jim and Clark strolled over toward the Ford, their shoes crunching raucously on the gravel drive.

"Oh boy!" sighed Clark softly, "how you can set those dice!"

It was still too dark for him to see the flush on Jim's thin cheeks—or to know that it was a flush of unfamiliar shame.

IV

Over Tilly's garage a bleak room echoed all day to the rumble and snorting downstairs and the singing of the negro washers as they turned the hose on the cars outside. It was a cheerless square of a room, punctuated with a bed and a battered table on which lay half a dozen books—Joe Miller's "Slow Train thru Arkansas"; "Lucille," in an old edition very much annotated in an old-fashioned hand; "The Eyes of the World," by Harold Bell Wright; and an ancient prayer-book of the Church of England with the name Alice Powell and the date 1831 written on the fly-leaf.

The east, gray when the Jelly-bean entered the garage, became a rich and vivid blue as he turned on his solitary electric light. He snapped it out again, and going to the window rested his elbows on the sill and stared into the deepening morning. With the awakening of his emotions, his first perception was a sense of futility, a dull ache at the utter grayness of his life. A wall had sprung up suddenly around him hedging him in, a wall as definite and tangible as the white wall of his bare room. And with his perception of this wall all that had been the romance of his existence, the casualness, the light-hearted improvidence, the miraculous open-handedness of life faded out. The Jelly-bean strolling up Jackson Street humming a lazy song, known at every shop and street stand, cropful of easy greeting and local wit, sad sometimes for only the sake of sadness and the flight of time—that Jelly-bean was suddenly vanished. The very name was a reproach, a triviality. With a flood of insight he knew that Merritt must despise him, that even Nancy's kiss in the dawn would have awakened not jealousy but only a contempt for Nancy's so lowering herself. And on his part the Jelly-bean had used for her a dingy subterfuge learned from the garage. He had been her moral laundry; the stains were his.

As the gray became blue, brightened and filled the room, he crossed to his bed and threw himself down on it, gripping the edges fiercely.

"I love her," he cried aloud. "God!"

As he said this something gave way within him like a lump melting in his throat. The air cleared and became radiant with dawn, and turning over on his face he began to sob dully into the pillow.

In the sunshine of three o'clock Clark Darrow chugging painfully along Jackson Street was hailed by the Jelly-bean, who stood on the curb with his fingers in his vest pockets.

"Hi!" called Clark, bringing his Ford to an astonishing stop alongside. "Just get up?"

The Jelly-bean shook his head.

"Never did go to bed. Felt sorta restless, so I took a long walk this morning out in the country. Just got into town this minute."

"Should think you *would* feel restless. I been feeling thataway all day——"

"I'm thinkin' of leavin' town," continued the Jelly-bean, absorbed by his own thoughts. "Been thinkin' of goin' up on the farm, and takin' a little that work off Uncle Dun. Reckin I been bummin' too long."

Clark was silent and the Jelly-bean continued:

"I reckin maybe after Aunt Mamie dies I could sink that money of mine in the farm and make somethin' out of it. All my people originally came from that part up there. Had a big place."

Clark looked at him curiously.

"That's funny," he said. "This—this sort of affected me the same way."

The Jelly-bean hesitated.

"I don't know," he began slowly, "somethin' about—about that girl last night talkin' about a lady named Diana Manners—an English lady, sorta got me thinkin'!" He drew himself up and looked oddly at Clark. "I had a family once," he said defiantly.

Clark nodded.

"I know."

"And I'm the last of 'em," continued the Jelly-bean, his voice rising slightly, "and I ain't worth shucks. Name they call me by means jelly—weak and wobbly like. People who weren't nothin' when my folks was a lot turn up their noses when they pass me on the street."

Again Clark was silent.

"So I'm through. I'm goin' today. And when I come back to this town it's going to be like a gentleman."

Clark took out his handkerchief and wiped his damp brow.

"Reckon you're not the only one it shook up," he admitted gloomily. "All this thing of girls going round like they do is going to stop right quick. Too bad, too, but everybody'll have to see it thataway."

"Do you mean," demanded Jim in surprise, "that all that's leaked out?"

"Leaked out? How on earth could they keep it secret? It'll be announced in the papers tonight. Doctor Lamar's got to save his name somehow."

Jim put his hands on the sides of the car and tightened his long fingers on the metal.

"Do you mean Taylor investigated those checks?"

It was Clark's turn to be surprised.

"Haven't you heard what happened?"

Jim's startled eyes were answer enough.

"Why," announced Clark dramatically, "those four got another bottle of corn, got tight and decided to shock the town—so Nancy and that fella Merritt were married in Rockville at seven o'clock this morning."

A tiny indentation appeared in the metal under the Jelly-bean's fingers.

"Married?"

"Sure enough. Nancy sobered up and rushed back into town, crying and frightened to death—claimed it'd all been a mistake. First Doctor Lamar went wild and was going to kill Merritt, but finally they got it patched up some way, and Nancy and Merritt went to Savannah on the two-thirty train."

Jim closed his eyes and with an effort overcame a sudden sickness.

"It's too bad," said Clark philosophically. "I don't mean the wedding—reckon that's all right, though I don't guess Nancy cared a darn about him. But it's a crime for a nice girl like that to hurt her family that way."

The Jelly-bean let go the car and turned away. Again something was going on inside him, some inexplicable but almost chemical change.

"Where you going?" asked Clark.

The Jelly-bean turned and looked dully back over his shoulder.

"Got to go," he muttered. "Been up too long; feelin' right sick."

"Oh."

The street was hot at three and hotter still at four, the April dust seeming to enmesh the sun and give it forth again as a world-old joke forever played on an eternity of afternoons. But at half past four a first layer of quiet fell and the shades lengthened under the awnings and heavy foliaged trees. In this heat nothing mattered. All life was weather, a waiting through the hot where events had no significance for the cool that was soft and caressing like a woman's hand on a tired forehead. Down in Georgia there is a feeling—perhaps inarticulate—that this is the greatest wisdom of the South—so after awhile the Jelly-bean turned into a pool-hall on Jackson Street where he was sure to find a congenial crowd who would make all the old jokes—the ones he knew.

The Last of the Belles

The Saturday Evening Post, 2 March 1929

AFTER ATLANTA's elaborate and theatrical rendition of Southern charm, we all underestimated Tarleton. It was a little hotter than anywhere we'd been—a dozen rookies collapsed the first day in that Georgia sun—and when you saw herds of cows drifting through the business streets, hi-yaed by colored drovers, a trance stole down over you out of the hot light; you wanted to move a hand or foot to be sure you were alive.

So I stayed out at camp and let Lieutenant Warren tell me about the girls. This was fifteen years ago, and I've forgotten how I felt, except that the days went along, one after another, better than they do now, and I was empty-hearted, because up North she whose legend I had loved for three years was getting married. I saw the clippings and newspaper photographs. It was "a romantic wartime wedding," all very rich and sad. I felt vividly the dark radiance of the sky under which it took place, and as a young snob, was more envious than sorry.

A day came when I went into Tarleton for a haircut and ran into a nice fellow named Bill Knowles, who was in my

ALL OF THE BELLES

time at Harvard. He'd been in the National Guard division that preceded us in camp; at the last moment he had transferred to aviation and been left behind.

"I'm glad I met you, Andy," he said with undue seriousness. "I'll hand you on all my information before I start for Texas. You see, there're really only three girls here—"

I was interested; there was something mystical about there being three girls.

"—and here's one of them now."

We were in front of a drug store and he marched me in and introduced me to a lady I promptly detested.

"The other two are Ailie Calhoun and Sally Carrol Happer."

I guessed from the way he pronounced her name that he was interested in Ailie Calhoun. It was on his mind what she would be doing while he was gone; he wanted her to have a quiet, uninteresting time.

At my age I don't even hesitate to confess that entirely unchivalrous images of Ailie Calhoun—that lovely name— rushed into my mind. At twenty-three there is no such thing as a preempted beauty; though, had Bill asked me, I would doubtless have sworn in all sincerity to care for her like a sister. He didn't; he was just fretting out loud at having to go. Three days later he telephoned me that he was leaving next morning and he'd take me to her house that night.

We met at the hotel and walked uptown through the flowery, hot twilight. The four white pillars of the Calhoun house faced the street, and behind them the verandah was dark as a cave with hanging, weaving, climbing vines.

When we came up the walk a girl in a white dress tumbled out of the front door, crying, "I'm so sorry I'm late!" and seeing us, added: "Why, I thought I heard you come ten minutes—"

She broke off as a chair creaked and another man, an aviator from Camp Harry Lee, emerged from the obscurity of the verandah.

"Why, Canby!" she cried. "How you?"

He and Bill Knowles waited with the tenseness of open litigants.

"Canby, I want to whisper to you, honey," she said, after just a second. "You'll excuse us, Bill."

They went aside. Presently Lieutenant Canby, immensely displeased, said in a grim voice, "Then we'll make it Thursday, but that means sure." Scarcely nodding to us, he went down the walk, the spurs with which he presumably urged on his aeroplane gleaming in the lamplight.

"Come in y'all,—I don't just know your name—"

There she was—the Southern type in all its purity. I would have recognized Ailie Calhoun if I'd never heard Ruth Draper or read "Marse Chan." She had the adroitness sugarcoated with sweet, voluble simplicity, the suggested background of devoted fathers, brothers and admirers stretching back into the South's heroic age, the unfailing coolness acquired in the endless struggle with the heat. There were notes in her voice that ordered slaves around, that withered up Yankee captains, and then soft, wheedling notes that mingled in unfamiliar loveliness with the night.

I could scarcely see her in the darkness, but when I rose

to go—it was plain that I was not to linger—she stood in the orange light from the doorway. She was small and very blonde; there was too much fever-colored rouge on her face, accentuated by a nose dabbed clownish white, but she shone through that like a star.

"After Bill goes I'll be sitting here all alone night after night. Maybe you'll take me to the country-club dances." The pathetic prophecy brought a laugh from Bill. "Wait a minute," Ailie murmured. "Your guns are all crooked."

She straightened my collar pin, looking up at me for a second with something more than curiosity. It was a seeking look, as if she asked, "Could it be you?" Like Lieutenant Canby, I marched off unwillingly into the suddenly insufficient night.

Two weeks later I sat with her on the same verandah, or rather she half lay in my arms and yet scarcely touched me—how she managed that I don't remember. I was trying unsuccessfully to kiss her and had been trying for the best part of an hour. We had a sort of joke about my not being sincere. My theory was that if she'd let me kiss her I'd fall in love with her. Her argument was that I was obviously insincere.

In a lull between two of these struggles she told me about her brother who had died in his senior year at Yale. She showed me his picture—it was a handsome, earnest face with a Leyendecker forelock—and told me that when she met someone who measured up to him she'd marry. I found this family idealism discouraging; even my brash confidence couldn't compete with the dead.

The evening and other evenings passed like that, and ended with my going back to camp with the remembered smell of magnolia flowers and a mood of vague dissatisfaction. I never kissed her. We went to the vaudeville and to the country club on Saturday nights, where she seldom took ten consecutive steps with one man, and she took me to barbecues and rowdy watermelon parties, and never thought it was worth while to change what I felt for her into love. I see now that it wouldn't have been hard, but she was a wise nineteen and she must have seen that we were emotionally incompatible. So I became her confidant instead.

We talked about Bill Knowles. She was considering Bill; for, though she wouldn't admit it, a winter at school in New York and a prom at Yale had turned her eyes North. She said she didn't think she'd marry a Southern man. And by degrees I saw that she was consciously and voluntarily different from these other girls who sang nigger songs and shot craps in the country-club bar. That's why Bill and I and others were drawn to her. We recognized her.

June and July, while the rumors reached us faintly, ineffectually, of battle and terror overseas, Ailie's eyes roved here and there about the country-club floor, seeking for something among the tall young officers. She attached several, choosing them with unfailing perspicacity—save in the case of Lieutenant Canby, whom she claimed to despise, but, nevertheless, gave dates to "because he was so sincere"—and we apportioned her evenings among us all summer.

One day she broke all her dates—Bill Knowles had leave

and was coming. We talked of the event with scientific impersonality—would he move her to a decision? Lieutenant Canby, on the contrary, wasn't impersonal at all; made a nuisance of himself. He told her that if she married Knowles he was going to climb up six thousand feet in his aeroplane, shut off the motor, and let go. He frightened her—I had to yield him my last date before Bill came.

On Saturday night she and Bill Knowles came to the country club. They were very handsome together and once more I felt envious and sad. As they danced out on the floor the three-piece orchestra was playing "After You've Gone," in a poignant incomplete way that I can hear yet, as if each bar were trickling off a precious minute of that time. I knew then that I had grown to love Tarleton, and I glanced about half in panic to see if some face wouldn't come in for me out of that warm, singing, outer darkness that yielded up couple after couple in organdie and olive drab. It was a time of youth and war, and there was never so much love around.

When I danced with Ailie she suddenly suggested that we go outside to a car. She wanted to know why didn't people cut in on her tonight? Did they think she was already married?

"Are you going to be?"

"I don't know, Andy. Sometimes, when he treats me as if I were sacred, it thrills me." Her voice was hushed and far away. "And then—"

She laughed. Her body, so frail and tender, was touching mine, her face was turned up to me, and there, suddenly, with Bill Knowles ten yards off, I could have kissed her at last. Our lips just touched experimentally; then an aviation officer turned a corner of the verandah near us, peered into our darkness, and hesitated.

"Ailie."

"Yes."

"You heard about this afternoon?"

"What?" She leaned forward, tenseness already in her voice.

"Horace Canby crashed. He was instantly killed."

She got up slowly and stepped out of the car.

"You mean he was killed?" she said.

"Yes. They don't know what the trouble was. His motor—"

"Oh-h-h!" Her rasping whisper came through the hands suddenly covering her face. We watched her helplessly as she put her head on the side of the car, gagging dry tears. After a minute I went for Bill, who was standing in the stag line, searching anxiously about for her, and told him she wanted to go home.

I sat on the steps outside. I had disliked Canby, but his terrible, pointless death was more real to me then than the day's toll of thousands in France. In a few minutes Ailie and Bill came out. Ailie was whimpering a little, but when she saw me her eyes flexed and she came over swiftly.

"Andy"—she spoke in a quick, low voice—"of course you must never tell anybody what I told you about Canby yesterday. What he said, I mean."

"Of course not."

She looked at me a second longer as if to be quite sure. Finally she was sure. Then she sighed in such a quaint little way that I could hardly believe my ears, and her brow went up in what can only be described as mock despair.

"*An*-dy!"

I looked uncomfortably at the ground, aware that she was calling my attention to her involuntarily disastrous effect on men.

"Good-night, Andy!" called Bill as they got into a taxi.

"Good-night," I said, and almost added: "You poor fool."

II

Of course I should have made one of those fine moral decisions that people make in books and despised her. On the contrary, I don't doubt that she could still have had me by raising her hand.

A few days later she made it all right by saying wistfully, "I know you think it was terrible of me to think of myself at a time like that, but it was such a shocking coincidence."

At twenty-three I was entirely unconvinced about anything, except that some people were strong and attractive and could do what they wanted, and others were caught and disgraced. I hoped I was of the former. I was sure Ailie was.

I had to revise other ideas about her. In the course of a long discussion with some girl about kissing—in those days people still talked about kissing more than they kissed—I mentioned the fact that Ailie had only kissed two or three men, and only when she thought she was in love. To my considerable disconcertion the girl figuratively just lay on the floor and howled.

"But it's true," I assured her, suddenly knowing it wasn't. "She told me herself."

"Ailie Calhoun! Oh, my heavens! Why, last year at the Tech spring house party—"

This was in September. We were going over-seas any week now, and to bring us up to full strength a last batch of officers from the fourth training camp arrived. The fourth camp wasn't like the first three—the candidates were from the ranks; even from the drafted divisions. They had queer names without vowels in them, and save for a few young militiamen, you couldn't take it for granted that they came out of any background at all. The addition to our company was Lieutenant Earl Schoen from New Bedford, Massachusetts; as fine a physical specimen as I have ever seen. He was six-foot-three, with black hair, high color, and glossy dark-brown eyes. He wasn't very smart and he was definitely illiterate, yet he was a good officer, high-tempered and commanding, and with that becoming touch of vanity that sits well on the military. I had an idea that New Bedford was a country town and set down his bumptious qualities to that.

We were doubled up in living quarters and he came into my hut. Inside of a week there was a cabinet photograph of some Tarleton girl nailed brutally to the shack wall.

"She's no jane or anything like that. She's a society girl; goes with all the best people here."

The following Sunday afternoon I met the lady at a

semi-private swimming pool in the country. When Ailie and I arrived, there was Schoen's muscular body rippling out of a bathing suit at the far end of the pool.

"Hey, lieutenant!"

When I waved back at him he grinned and winked, jerking his head toward the girl at his side. Then, digging her in the ribs, he jerked his head at me. It was a form of introduction.

"Who's that with Kitty Preston?" Ailie asked, and when I told her she said he looked like a street-car conductor, and pretended to look for her transfer.

A moment later he crawled powerfully and gracefully down the pool and pulled himself up at our side. I introduced him to Ailie.

"How do you like my girl, lieutenant?" he demanded. "I told you she was all right, didn't I?" He jerked his head toward Ailie, this time to indicate that his girl and Ailie moved in the same circles. "How about let's us all having dinner together down at the hotel some night?"

I left them in a moment, amused as I saw Ailie visibly making up her mind that here, anyhow, was not the ideal. But Lieutenant Earl Schoen was not to be dismissed so lightly. He ran his eyes cheerfully and inoffensively over her cute, slight figure, and decided that she would do even better than the other. Then minutes later I saw them in the water together, Ailie swimming away with a grim little stroke she had, and Schoen wallowing riotously around her and ahead of her, sometimes pausing and staring at her, fascinated, as a boy might look at a nautical doll.

While the afternoon passed he remained at her side. Finally Ailie came over to me and whispered, with a laugh: "He's following me around. He thinks I haven't paid my carfare."

She turned quickly. Miss Kitty Preston, her face curiously flustered, stood facing us.

"Ailie Calhoun, I didn't think it of you to go out and delib'ately try to take a man away from another girl."

An expression of distress at the impending scene flitted over Ailie's face.

"I thought you considered yourself above anything like that," continued Kitty.

Her voice was low, but it held that tensity that can be felt farther than it can be heard, and I saw Ailie's clear lovely eyes glance about in panic. Luckily, Earl himself was ambling cheerfully and innocently toward us.

"If you care for him you certainly oughtn't to belittle yourself in front of him," said Ailie in a flash, her head high.

It was her acquaintance with the traditional way of behaving against Kitty Preston's naïve and fierce possessiveness, or if you prefer it, Ailie's "breeding" against the other's "commonness." She turned away.

"Wait a minute, kid!" cried Earl Schoen. "How about your address? Maybe I'd like to give you a ring on the phone."

She looked at him in a way that should have indicated to Kitty her entire lack of interest.

"I'm very busy at the Red Cross this month," she said, her voice as cool as her slicked-back blonde hair. "Good-bye."

On the way home she laughed. Her air of having been unwittingly involved in a contemptible business vanished.

"She'll never hold that young man," she said. "He wants somebody new."

"Apparently he wants Ailie Calhoun."

The idea amused her.

"He could give me his ticket punch to wear, like a fraternity pin. What fun! If mother ever saw anybody like that come in the house, she'd just lay down and die."

And to give Ailie credit, it was fully a fortnight before he did come in her house, although he rushed her until she pretended to be annoyed at the next country-club dance.

"He's the biggest tough, Andy," she whispered to me. "But he's so sincere."

She used the word "tough" without the conviction it would have carried had he been a Southern boy. She only knew it with her mind; her ear couldn't distinguish between one Yankee voice and another. And somehow Mrs. Calhoun didn't expire at his appearance on the threshold. The supposedly ineradicable prejudices of Ailie's parents were a convenient phenomenon that disappeared at her wish. It was her friends who were astonished. Ailie, always a little above Tarleton, whose beaux had been very carefully the "nicest" men of the camp—Ailie and Lieutenant Schoen! I grew tired of assuring people that she was merely distracting herself—and indeed every week or so there was someone new—an ensign from Pensacola, an old friend from New Orleans—but always, in between times, there was Earl Schoen.

Orders arrived for an advance party of officers and sergeants to proceed to the port of embarkation and take ship to France. My name was on the list. I had been on the range for a week and when I got back to camp, Earl Schoen buttonholed me immediately.

"We're giving a little farewell party in the mess. Just you and I and Captain Craker and three girls."

Earl and I were to call for the girls. We picked up Sally Carrol Happer and Nancy Lamar, and went on to Ailie's house, to be met at the door by the butler with the announcement that she wasn't home.

"Isn't home?" Earl repeated blankly. "Where is she?"

"Didn't leave no information about that; just said she wasn't home."

"But this is a darn funny thing!" he exclaimed. He walked around the familiar dusky verandah while the butler waited at the door. Something occurred to him. "Say," he informed me—"say, I think she's sore."

I waited. He said sternly to the butler, "You tell her I've got to speak to her a minute."

"How'm I goin' tell her that when she ain't home?"

Again Earl walked musingly around the porch. Then he nodded several times and said:

"She's sore at something that happened downtown."

In a few words he sketched out the matter to me.

"Look here; you wait in the car," I said. "Maybe I can fix this." And when he reluctantly retreated: "Oliver, you tell Miss Ailie I want to see her alone."

After some argument he bore this message and in a moment returned with a reply:

"Miss Ailie say she don't want to see that other gentleman about nothing never. She say come in if you like."

She was in the library. I had expected to see a picture of cool, outraged dignity, but her face was distraught, tumultuous, despairing. Her eyes were red-rimmed, as though she had been crying slowly and painfully, for hours.

"Oh, hello, Andy," she said brokenly. "I haven't seen you for so long. Has he gone?"

"Now, Ailie—"

"Now, Ailie!" she cried. "Now, Ailie! He spoke to me, you see. He lifted his hat. He stood there ten feet from me with that horrible—that horrible woman—holding her arm and talking to her, and then when he saw me he raised his hat. Andy, I didn't know what to do. I had to go in the drug store and ask for a glass of water, and I was so afraid he'd follow in after me that I asked Mr. Rich to let me go out the back way. I never want to see him or hear of him again."

I talked. I said what one says in such cases. I said it for half an hour. I could not move her. Several times she answered by murmuring something about his not being "sincere," and for the fourth time I wondered what the word meant to her. Certainly not constancy; it was, I half suspected, some special way she wanted to be regarded.

I got up to go. And then, unbelievably, the automobile horn sounded three times impatiently outside. It was stupefying. It said as plainly as if Earl were in the room, "All right, go to the devil then! I'm not going to wait here all night."

Ailie looked at me aghast. And suddenly a peculiar look came into her face, spread, flickered, broke into a teary, hysterical smile.

"Isn't he awful?" she cried in helpless despair. "Isn't he terrible?"

"Hurry up," I said quickly. "Get your cape. This is our last night."

And I can still feel that last night vividly, the candlelight that flickered over the rough boards of the mess shack, over the frayed paper decorations left from the supply company's party, the sad mandolin down a company street that kept picking "My Indiana Home" out of the universal nostalgia of the departing summer. The three girls lost in this mysterious men's city felt something, too—a bewitched impermanence as though they were on a magic carpet that had lighted on the Southern countryside, and any moment the wind would lift it and waft it away. We toasted ourselves and the South. Then we left our napkins and empty glasses and a little of the past on the table, and hand in hand went out into the moonlight itself. Taps had been played; there was no sound but the far-away whinny of a horse, and a loud persistent snore at which we laughed, and the leathery snap of a sentry coming to port over by the guardhouse. Craker was on duty; we others got into a waiting car, motored into Tarleton and left Craker's girl.

Then Ailie and Earl, Sally and I, two and two in the wide back seat, each couple turned from the other, absorbed and whispering, drove away into the wide, flat darkness.

We drove through pine woods heavy with lichen and Spanish moss, and between the fallow cotton fields along a road white as the rim of the world. We parked under the broken shadow of a mill where there was the sound of running water and restive squawky birds and over everything a brightness that tried to filter in anywhere—into the lost nigger cabins, the automobile, the fastnesses of the heart. The South sang to us—I wonder if they remember. I remember—the cool pale faces, the somnolent amorous eyes and the voices:

"Are you comfortable?"

"Yes, are you?"

"Are you sure you are?"

"Yes."

Suddenly we knew it was late and there was nothing more. We turned home.

Our detachment started for Camp Mills next day, but I didn't go to France after all. We passed a cold month on Long Island, marched aboard a transport with steel helmets slung at our sides and then marched off again. There wasn't any more war. I had missed the war. When I came back to Tarleton I tried to get out of the Army, but I had a regular commission and it took most of the winter. But Earl Schoen was one of the first to be demobilized. He wanted to find a good job "while the picking was good." Ailie was noncommittal, but there was an understanding between them that he'd be back.

By January the camps, which for two years had dominated the little city, were already fading. There was only the persistent incinerator smell to remind one of all that activity and bustle. What life remained centered bitterly about divisional headquarters building, with the disgruntled regular officers who had also missed the war.

And now the young men of Tarleton began drifting back from the ends of the earth—some with Canadian uniforms, some with crutches or empty sleeves. A returned battalion of the National Guard paraded through the streets with open ranks for their dead, and then stepped down out of romance forever and sold you things over the counters of local stores. Only a few uniforms mingled with the dinner coats at the country-club dance.

Just before Christmas, Bill Knowles arrived unexpectedly one day and left the next—either he gave Ailie an ultimatum or she had made up her mind at last. I saw her sometimes when she wasn't busy with returned heroes from Savannah and Augusta, but I felt like an outmoded survival—and I was. She was waiting for Earl Schoen with such a vast uncertainty that she didn't like to talk about it. Three days before I got my final discharge he came.

I first happened upon them walking down Market Street together, and I don't think I've ever been so sorry for a couple in my life—though I suppose the same situation was repeating itself in every city where there had been camps. Exteriorly Earl had about everything wrong with him that could be imagined. His hat was green, with a radical feather; his suit was slashed and braided in a grotesque fashion that national advertising and the movies have put an end to. Evidently he had been to his old barber, for his hair bloused neatly on his pink, shaved neck. It wasn't as though he had been shiny and poor, but the background of mill-town dance halls and outing clubs flamed out at you—or rather flamed out at Ailie. For she had never quite imagined the reality; in these clothes even the natural grace of that magnificent body had departed. At first he boasted of his fine job; it would get them along all right until he could "see some easy money." But from the moment he came back into her world on its own terms he must have known it was hopeless. I don't know what Ailie said or how much her grief weighed against her stupefaction. She acted quickly—three days after his arrival, Earl and I went north together on the train.

"Well, that's the end of that," he said moodily. "She's a wonderful girl, but too much of a highbrow for me. I guess she's got to marry some rich guy that'll give her a great social position. I can't see that stuck-up sort of thing." And then, later: "She said to come back and see her in a year, but I'll never go back. This aristocrat stuff is all right if you got the money for it, but—"

"But it wasn't real," he meant to finish. The provincial society in which he had moved with so much satisfaction for six months already appeared to him as affected, "dude-ish," and artificial.

"Say, did you see what I saw getting on the train?" he asked me after awhile. "Two wonderful janes, all alone. What do you say we mosey into the next car and ask them to lunch? I'll take the one in blue." Halfway down the car he turned around suddenly. "Say, Andy," he demanded, frowning; "one thing—how do you suppose she knew I used to command a street car? I never told her that."

"Search me."

III

This narrative arrives now at one of the big gaps that stared me in the face when I began. For six years, while I finished at Harvard Law and built commercial aeroplanes and backed a pavement block that went gritty under trucks, Ailie Calhoun was scarcely more than a name on a Christmas card, something that blew a little in my mind on warm nights when I remembered the magnolia flowers. Occasionally an acquaintance of Army days would ask me, "What became of that blonde girl who was so popular?" but I didn't know. I ran into Nancy Lamar at the Montmartre in New York one evening and learned that Ailie had become engaged to a man in Cincinnati, had gone north to visit his family, and then broken it off. She was lovely as ever and there was always a heavy beau or two. But neither Bill Knowles nor Earl Schoen had ever come back.

And somewhere about that time I heard that Bill Knowles had married a girl he met on a boat. There you are—not much of a patch to mend six years with.

Oddly enough, a girl seen at twilight in a small Indiana station started me thinking about going south. The girl, in stiff pink organdie, threw her arms about a man who got off our train and hurried him to a waiting car, and I felt a sort of pang. It seemed to me that she was bearing him off into the lost midsummer world of my early twenties, where time had stood still and charming girls, dimly seen like the past itself, still loitered along the dusky streets. I suppose that poetry is a Northern man's dream of the South. But it was months later that I sent off a wire to Ailie, and immediately followed it to Tarleton.

It was July. The Jefferson Hotel seemed strangely shabby and stuffy—a boosters' club burst into intermittent song in the dining room that my memory had long dedicated to officers and girls. I recognized the taxi driver who took me up to Ailie's house, but his "Sure, I do, lieutenant," was unconvincing. I was only one of twenty thousand.

It was a curious three days. I suppose some of Ailie's first young luster must have gone the way of such mortal shining, but I can't bear witness to it. She was still so physically appealing that you wanted to touch the personality that trembled on her lips. No—the change was more profound than that.

At once I saw she had a different line. The modulations of pride, the vocal hints that she knew the secrets of a brighter, finer ante-bellum day, were gone from her voice; there was no time for them now as it rambled on in the half-laughing, half-desperate banter of the newer South. And everything was swept into this banter in order to make it go on and leave no time for thinking—the present, the future, herself, me. We went to a rowdy party at the house of some young married people, and she was the nervous, glowing center of it. After all, she wasn't eighteen, and she was as attractive in her role of reckless clown as she had ever been in her life.

"Have you heard anything from Earl Schoen?" I asked her the second night, on our way to the country-club dance.

"No." She was serious for a moment. "I often think of him. He was the—" She hesitated.

"Go on."

"I was going to say the man I loved most, but that wouldn't be true. I never exactly loved him, or I'd have married him any old how, wouldn't I?" She looked at me questioningly. "At least I wouldn't have treated him like that."

"It was impossible."

"Of course," she agreed uncertainly. Her mood changed; she became flippant: "How the Yankees did deceive us poor little Southern girls. Ah, me!"

When we reached the country club she melted like a chameleon into the—to me—unfamiliar crowd. There was a new generation upon the floor, with less dignity than the ones I had known, but none of them were more a part of its lazy, feverish essence than Ailie. Possibly she had perceived that in her initial longing to escape from Tarleton's provincialism she had been walking alone, following a generation which was doomed to have no successors. Just where she lost the battle, waged behind the white pillars of her verandah, I don't know. But she had guessed wrong, missed out somewhere. Her wild animation, which even now called enough men around her to rival the entourage of the youngest and freshest, was an admission of defeat.

I left her house, as I had so often left it that vanished June, in a mood of vague dissatisfaction. It was hours later, tossing about my bed in the hotel, that I realized what was the matter, what had always been the matter—I was deeply and incurably in love with her. In spite of every incompatibility, she was still, she would always be to me, the most attractive girl I had ever known. I told her so next afternoon. It was one of those hot days I knew so well, and Ailie sat beside me on a couch in the darkened library.

"Oh, no, I couldn't marry you," she said, almost frightened; "I don't love you that way at all. . . . I never did. And you don't love me. I didn't mean to tell you now, but next month I'm going to marry another man. We're not even announcing it, because I've done that twice before." Suddenly it occurred to her that I might be hurt: "Andy, you just had a silly idea, didn't you? You know I couldn't ever marry a Northern man."

"Who is he?" I demanded.

"A man from Savannah."

"Are you in love with him?"

"Of course I am." We both smiled. "Of *course* I am! What are you trying to make me say?"

There were no doubts, as there had been with other men. She couldn't afford to let herself have doubts. I knew this because she had long ago stopped making any pretensions with me. This very naturalness, I realized, was because she didn't consider me as a suitor. Beneath her mask of an instinctive thoroughbred she had always been on to herself, and she couldn't believe that anyone not taken in to the point of uncritical worship could really love her. That was what she called being "sincere"; she felt most security with men like Canby and Earl Schoen, who were incapable of passing judgments on the ostensibly aristocratic heart.

"All right," I said, as if she had asked my permission to marry. "Now, would you do something for me?"

"Anything."

"Ride out to camp."

"But there's nothing left there, honey."

"I don't care."

We walked downtown. The taxi driver in front of the hotel repeated her objection: "Nothing there now, cap."

"Never mind. Go there anyhow."

Twenty minutes later he stopped on a wide unfamiliar plain powdered with new cotton fields and marked with isolated clumps of pine.

"Like to drive over yonder where you see the smoke?" asked the driver. "That's the new state prison."

"No. Just drive along this road. I want to find where I used to live."

An old race course, inconspicuous in the camp's day of glory, had reared its dilapidated grandstand in the desolation. I tried in vain to orient myself.

"Go along this road past that clump of trees, and then turn right—no, turn left."

He obeyed, with professional disgust.

"You won't find a single thing, darling," said Ailie. "The contractors took it all down."

We rode slowly along the margin of the fields. It might have been here—

"All right. I want to get out," I said suddenly.

I left Ailie sitting in the car, looking very beautiful with the warm breeze stirring her long, curly bob.

It might have been here. That would make the company streets down there and the mess shack, where we dined that night, just over the way.

The taxi driver regarded me indulgently while I stumbled here and there in the knee-deep underbrush, looking for my youth in a clapboard or a strip of roofing or a rusty tomato can. I tried to sight on a vaguely familiar clump of trees, but it was growing darker now and I couldn't be quite sure they were the right trees.

"They're going to fix up the old race course," Ailie called from the car. "Tarleton's getting quite doggy in its old age."

No. Upon consideration they didn't look like the right trees. All I could be sure of was this place that had once been so full of life and effort was gone, as if it had never existed, and that in another month Ailie would be gone, and the South would be empty for me forever.